"I've just taken down *Miami Blues* in one fevered gulp and must tell you that it is absolutely brilliant in every regard—the definitive Miami novel."

Stanley Ellin

"Bone-deep satire . . . a harrowing and surprisingly amusing story . . . a terrific thriller."

Publishers Weekly

"A nasty crime-comedy that's full of casual violence, outrageous coincidences, and hilariously rude dialogue . . . Willeford has a marvelously deadpan way with losers on both sides of the law."

The Kirkus Reviews

MIAMI *Blues*

MIAMI Blues

CHARLES WILLEFORD

BALLANTINE BOOKS • NEW YORK

Library of Congress Catalog Card Number: 83-17692

ISBN 0-345-32016-6

This edition published by arrangement with St. Martin's Press.

Manufactured in the United States of America

First Ballantine Books Edition: May 1985
Seventh Printing: November 1989

For Betsy

Haiku

Morning sun stripes cell.
Five fingers feel my hard heart.
It hurts, hurts, like hell.

—F. J. Frenger, Jr.

1

FREDERICK J. FRENGER, JR., a blithe psychopath from California, asked the flight attendant in first class for another glass of champagne and some writing materials. She brought him a cold half-bottle, uncorked it and left it with him, and returned a few moments later with some Pan Am writing paper and a white ball point pen. For the next hour, as he sipped champagne, Freddy practiced writing the signatures of Claude L. Bytell, Ramon Mendez, and Herman T. Gotlieb.

The signatures on his collection of credit cards, driver's licenses, and other ID cards were difficult to imitate, but by the end of the hour and the champagne, when it was time for lunch—martini, small steak, baked potato, salad, chocolate cake, and two glasses of red wine—Freddy decided that he was close enough to the originals to get by.

The best way to forge a signature, he knew, was to turn it upside down and draw it instead of trying to imitate the handwriting. That was the foolproof way, if a man had the time and the privacy and was forging a document or a check. But to use stolen credit cards, he knew he had to sign charge slips casually, in front of clerks and store managers who might be alert for irregularities.

Still, close enough was usually good enough for Freddy. He was not a careful person, and a full hour was a long time for him to engage in any activity without his mind turning to something else. As he looked through the three wallets he found himself wondering about their owners. One wallet was eelskin, another was imitation ostrich, and the third was a plain cowhide billfold filled with color snapshots of very plain children. Why would any man want to carry around photographs of ugly children in his wallet? And why would anyone buy imitation ostrich, when you could get an authentic ostrich-skin wallet for only two or three hundred dollars more? Eelskin he could understand; it was soft and durable, and the longer you carried it in your hip pocket the softer it got. He decided to keep the eelskin one. He crammed all of the credit cards and IDs into it, along with the photos of the ugly children, and shoved the two emptied wallets into the pocket of the seat in front of him, behind the in-flight magazine.

Comfortably full, and a trifle dizzy from the martini and the wine, Freddy stretched out in the wide reclining seat, hugging the tiny airline pillow. He slept soundly until the attendant awakened him gently and asked him to fasten his seat belt for the descent into Miami International Airport.

FREDDY HAD NO baggage, so he wandered through the mammoth airport listening to the announcements that boomed from multiple speakers, first in Spanish and then, half as long, in English. He was eager to get a cab and to find a hotel, but he also wanted some nice-looking luggage. Two pieces would be better than one, but he would settle for a Vuitton one-suiter if he could find one. He paused for a moment to light a Winston and reconnoiter a long line of American tourists and diminutive Indian men and women going to the Yucatán Peninsula. The vacationers kept very close to their baggage, and the Indians pushed along large boxes held together with strips of gray duct tape. Nothing for him there.

2

A Hare Krishna, badly disguised in jeans, a sports shirt, and a powder blue sports jacket, his head covered with an ill-fitting brown wig, stepped up to Freddy and pinned a red-and-white-striped piece of stick candy to Freddy's gray suede sports jacket. As the pin went into the lapel of the $287 jacket, charged the day before to a Claude L. Bytell at Macy's in San Francisco, Freddy was seized with a sudden rage. He could take the pin out, of course, but he knew that the tiny pinhole would be there forever because of this asshole's carelessness.

"I want to be your friend," the Hare Krishna said, "and—"

Freddy grasped the Hare Krishna's middle finger and bent it back sharply. The Krishna yelped. Freddy applied sharper pressure and jerked the finger backward, breaking it. The Krishna screamed, a high-pitched gargling sound, and collapsed onto his knees. Freddy let go of the dangling finger, and as the Krishna bent over, screaming, his wig fell off, exposing his shaved head.

Two men, obviously related, who had watched the whole encounter, broke into applause and laughed. When a middle-aged woman wearing a Colombian poncho heard one of the tourists say "Hare Krishna," she took a Krishna Kricket out of her purse and began to click the metal noisemaker in the pain-racked Krishna's face. The injured Krishna's partner, dressed similarly but wearing a black wig, came over from the line he was working at Aéromexico and began to berate the woman for snapping the Kricket. The elder of the two laughing men came up behind him, snatched off his wig, and threw it over the heads of the gathering crowd.

Freddy, who had slipped away from the scene, went into the men's room next to the bar on Concourse D and took the stick of candy out of his lapel. In a mirror he examined the pinhole and smoothed it out. A stranger would never notice it, he decided, but the flaw was there, even though it wasn't as bad as he had thought it would be. Freddy dropped the stick of candy into his jacket pocket, took a quick leak, washed his hands, and walked out.

A YOUNG WOMAN slept soundly in a row of hard-plastic airport chairs. A two-year-old boy sat beside her quietly, hugging a toy panda. The wide-eyed child, drooling slightly, had his feet resting on a one-suiter with the Cardin logo repeated on its light blue fabric. Freddy stopped in front of the boy, unwrapped the stick of candy, and offered it to him with a smile. The boy smiled back, took the candy shyly, and put one end in his mouth. As the boy sucked it, Freddy took the suitcase and walked away. He took the Down escalator to the outside ramp and hailed a Yellow cab. The Cuban driver, who spoke little English, finally smiled and nodded when Freddy said simply, "Hotel. Miami."

The cabbie lit a cigarette with his right hand and swung into the heavy traffic with his left, narrowly missing an old lady and her granddaughter. He cut in front of a Toyota, making the driver stall his engine, and headed for the Dolphin Expressway. By this route he managed to get Freddy into downtown Miami and to the front of the International Hotel in twenty-two minutes. The meter read $8.37. Freddy gave the driver a ten, handed his suitcase to the doorman, and registered at the desk as Herman T. Gotlieb, San Jose, California, using Gotlieb's credit card. He took a $135-a-day suite and signed the charge slip in advance, then followed the fat Latin bellman to the elevator. Just before the elevator reached the seventh floor, the bellman spoke up:

"If there's anything you want, Mr. Gotlieb, please let me know."

"I can't think of anything right now."

"What I mean . . ." the bellman cleared his throat.

"I understand what you're saying, but I don't want a girl right now."

The bedroom was small, but the sitting room was

furnished pleasantly with a comfortable couch and an easy chair in matching blue-and-white stripes, a desk with a glass top, and a small bar with two stools. The refrigerator behind the bar held vodka, gin, Scotch, and bourbon, several rows of mixers, and a split of champagne. There was a price list taped to the door. Freddy looked at the list and thought that the per-drink prices were outrageous. He gave the bellman $2.

"Thank you, sir. And if you need me for anything at all, just call down to the bell captain and ask for Pablo."

"Pablo. Fine. Where's the beach, Pablo? I might want to go for a swim later."

"The beach? We're on Biscayne Bay, sir, not the ocean. The ocean's over there in Miami Beach. But we have a nice pool on the roof, and a sauna. And if you want a massage—"

"No, that's okay. I just thought that Miami was on the ocean."

"No, sir. That's Miami Beach. They're separate cities, sir, connected by causeways. You wouldn't like it over there anyway, sir—it's nothing but crime on the Beach."

"You mean Miami isn't?"

"Not here, not on Brickell Avenue, anyway. This is the fattest part of Fat City."

"I noticed some shops off the lobby. Can I buy some trunks there?"

"I'll get you a pair, sir. What size?"

"Never mind. I'll do some shopping later."

The bellman left, and Freddy opened the draperies. He could see the towering AmeriFirst building, a part of the bay, the bridge across the Miami River, and the skyscrapers on Flagler Street. The street he was on, Brickell, was lined with mirrored, shimmering buildings. The air conditioning hummed quietly.

He had at least a week before the credit card numbers would be traced, but he didn't intend to stay in the International Hotel for more than one day. From now on he was going to play things a little safer, unless, of course, he wanted something. If he wanted something right away, that was a different matter altogether. But what he wanted this time, before he was caught, was to have some fun and to do some of the things he had wanted to do during his three years in San Quentin.

So far, he liked the clean white look of Miami, but he was astonished to learn that the city was not on the ocean.

2

THE VIP ROOM—or Golden Lounge, as it was sometimes called, after the gold plastic cards issued to first-class passengers by the three airlines that maintained it—was unusually crowded. The dead man lying on the blue carpet was not the only one who was there without a gold card.

Sergeant Hoke Moseley, Homicide, Miami Police Department, filled a Styrofoam cup with free coffee—his third—picked up a glazed doughnut from the assortment on the clear plastic tray and put it back, then doctored his coffee with Sweet 'n Low and N-Rich Coffee Creamer. Sergeant Bill Henderson, Hoke's hefty partner, sat on a royal blue couch and read John Keasler's humor column in *The Miami News*. Two middle-aged airport security men in electric blue sports jackets stood by the door, looking as if they were ready to take orders from anybody.

A black airport public relations man, wearing a hundred-dollar brown silk sports shirt and yellow linen golf slacks, was making notes with a gold pencil in a leather notebook. He put the notebook into his hip pocket and crossed the blue-carpeted room to talk to two men who said they were from Waycross, Georgia, John and Irwin Peeples. They glowered at him.

"Don't worry," the PR man said. "As soon as the state attorney gets here, and I've had a chance to talk to him, you'll be on the next flight out for Atlanta. And a plane of some kind leaves for Atlanta every half-hour."

"We don't want no plane of *some* kind," John Peeples said. "Me and Irwin fly Delta or nothing."

"No problem. If we have to, we'll bump a couple and get you on Delta inside of an hour."

"If I was you," Bill Henderson butted in, taking off his black-rimmed reading glasses, "I wouldn't promise these crackers anything. What we may be dealing with here is a Murder Two. For all I know, this whole thing might be a religious plot to murder that Krishna, with the two crackers in on it from the beginning. Ain't that right, Hoke?"

"I don't know yet," Hoke said. "Let's wait and see what the medical examiner and the state attorney have to say. At the least, Mr. and Mr. Peeples, you've got a long session ahead of you. We'll be wanting to talk to you downtown, and there'll be depositions to make out. As material witnesses to the"—he pointed to the body on the floor—"demise of this Krishna here, the state attorney might decide to keep you in Miami under protective custody for several months."

The brothers groaned. Hoke winked at Bill Henderson as he joined him on the couch.

The other Hare Krishna, the partner of the dead man, started to cry again. Someone had given him back his wig and he had stuffed it into his jacket pocket. He was at least twenty-five, but he looked much younger as he stifled his sobs and wiped his eyes with his fingertips. His freshly shaved head glistened with perspiration. He had never seen a dead person before, and here was his "brother," a man he had prayed with and eaten brown rice with, as dead as anyone could ever be, stretched out on the blue carpet of the VIP Room, and covered—except for feet in white cotton socks and scuffed Hush Puppies—with a cream-colored Aeroméxico blanket.

Dr. Merle Evans, the medical examiner, arrived with Violet Nygren, a blond and rather plain young assistant prosecutor from the state attorney's office. Hoke nodded to the security men at the door, and the two were let through. Hoke and Bill Henderson shook hands with Doc Evans, and the four of them moved to the back of the lounge, out of earshot of the Peeples', the PR man, and the weepy Krishna.

"I'm new on the beat," Violet Nygren said, as she introduced herself. "I've only been in the state attorney's office since I finished up at the UM Law School last June. But I'm willing to learn, Sergeant Moseley."

Hoke grinned. "Fair enough. This is my partner, Sergeant Henderson. If you're an attorney, Miss Nygren, where's your briefcase?"

"I've got a tape recorder in my purse," she said, holding up her leather drawstring bag.

"I was kidding. I've got a lot of respect for lady lawyers. My ex-wife had one, and I've been paying half my salary for alimony and child support for the last ten years."

"I haven't been on a homicide up to now," she said. "My caseloads so far have been mostly muggings and holdups. But, as I said, I'm here to learn, Sergeant."

"This may not *be* a homicide. That's why we wanted someone from the state attorney's office to come down with Doc Evans. We hope it isn't. We've had enough this year as it is. But that'll be up to you and Doc Evans to decide."

"That's awfully deferential, for you, Hoke," Doc Evans said. "What's bothering you?"

"Here's what happened. The body under the blanket's a Hare Krishna." Hoke looked at his opened notebook. "His name's Martin Waggoner, and his parents, according to that other Krishna over there, live in Okeechobee. He came down to Miami nine or ten months ago, joined the Krishnas, and they both reside in the new Krishna ashram out on Krome Avenue in the East 'Glades. These two have been working the airport for about six months, their regular assignment. The airport security people know them, and

9

they've been warned a couple of times about bothering the passengers. The dead man had more than two hundred dollars in his wallet, and the other Krishna's got about one-fifty. That's how much they've begged out here since seven A.M." Hoke looked at his wristwatch. "It's only twelve-forty-five now, and the Krishna over there said they usually take in about five hundred a day between them."

"Pretty good money." Violet Nygren raised her pale eyebrows. "I wouldn't have guessed they collected so much."

"The security people said there're two more Krishna teams working the airport besides this one. We haven't notified the commune, and we haven't called the Krishna's parents up in Okeechobee, yet."

"You haven't told us a hell of a lot, either," Doc Evans said.

"Our problem, Doc, is witnesses. There were maybe thirty witnesses, all in line at Aeroméxico, but they took the flight to Mérida. We managed to snag these two boys over there"—Hoke pointed to the Georgians, who looked to be in their forties—"but only because the uglier one on the right stole the victim's wig. The airline employees behind the counter said they didn't see anything. They were too busy, they said, and at check-in time I suppose they were. I got their names, and we can talk to them again later."

"Too bad," Henderson said, "that we couldn't find the lady with the Krishna Kricket."

"What's a Krishna Kricket?" Violet Nygren asked.

"They sell 'em out here in the bookshops and drugstores. It's just a metal cricket with a piece of spring steel inside. You click it at the Krishnas when they start bugging you. The noise usually drives them away. There used to be a Krishna-hater out here who gave them away free, but he ran out of crickets or money or ardor—I don't know. Anyway, the two brothers over there said she was closest to the action, and she kept clicking her Kricket at the Krishna until he stopped screaming."

10

"How was he killed?" Doc Evans said. "Or do you want me to look at him now and tell you? I've got to get back to the morgue."

"That's the point," Hoke said. "He wasn't actually killed. He bothered some guy wearing a leather coat. The guy bent his finger back and broke it. Then the guy walked away and disappeared. The Krishna went down on his knees, started screaming, and then, maybe five or six minutes later, he's dead. The security men brought his body in here, and the PR man over there called Homicide. So there it is—the Krishna died from a broken finger. How about it, Miss Nygren? Is that a homicide or not?"

"I never heard of anybody dying from a broken finger," she said.

"He must have died from shock," Doc Evans said. "I'll tell you for sure after I've had a look at him. How old is he, Hoke?"

"Twenty-one—according to his driver's license."

"That's what I mean," Doc Evans said, compressing his lips. "Young people today just can't stand up to pain the way we could when we were younger. This one was probably malnourished and in lousy shape. The pain was unexpected and just too much for him. It hurts like hell to have your finger bent back."

"You're telling me," Violet Nygren said. "My brother used to do it to me when I was a kid."

"And if you bend it back all the way," Doc Evans said, "until it breaks, it hurts like a son of a bitch. So he probably went into shock. Nobody gave him hot tea or covered him up with a blanket, and that was it. It doesn't take very long to die from shock."

"About five or six minutes, the Peeples brothers say."

"That's pretty fast," Doc Evans shook his head. "Shock usually takes fifteen or twenty minutes. But I'm not making any guesses. For all I know, without examining the body, there could be a bullet hole in him."

"I don't think so," Bill Henderson said. "All I saw was

11

the broken finger, and it's broken clean off—just hanging there."

"If it was an accident," Violet Nygren said, "it could still be simple assault. On the other hand, if the man in the leather jacket intended to kill him this way, knowing that there was a history of people dying from shock in the Krishna's background, this could very well be Murder One."

"That's really reaching for it," Hoke said. "You'll have to settle for manslaughter I think."

"I'm not so sure," she continued. "If you shoot a man and he dies later on from complications caused by the bullet, even though he was barely wounded when shot, we change the charge to either Murder One or Murder Two. I'll have to research this case, that's all. We can't do anything about it anyway until you catch the man in the leather jacket."

"That's all we've got to go on," Hoke said. "Leather jacket. We don't even know the *color* of the jacket. One guy said he had heard it was tan; another guy said he'd heard gray. Unless the man comes forward by himself, we haven't got a chance in hell of finding him. He could be on a plane for England or someplace at this minute." Hoke took a Kool out of a crumpled package, lit it, took one drag, and then butted it out in a standing ashtray. "The body's all yours, Doc. We've got all of the stuff out of his pockets."

Violet Nygren opened her purse and turned off her tape recorder. "I should tell my mom about this case," she said. "When my brother used to bend my fingers back, she never did anything to him." She laughed nervously. "Now I can tell her he was just trying to kill me."

3

FREDERICK J. FRENGER, JR., who preferred to be called
Junior instead of Freddy, was twenty-eight years old. He
looked older because his life had been a hard one; the lines
at the corners of his mouth seemed too deep for a man in his
late twenties. His eyes were a dark shade of blue, and his
untrimmed blond eyebrows were almost white. His nose
had been broken and reset poorly, but some women
considered him attractive. His skin was unblemished and
deeply tanned from long afternoons spent in the yard at San
Quentin. At five-nine, he should have had a slighter build,
but prolonged sessions with weights, pumping iron in the
yard, as well as playing handball, had built up his chest,
shoulders, and arms to almost grotesque proportions. He
had developed his stomach muscles to the point that he
could stand arms akimbo, and roll them in waves.

Freddy had been given a sentence of five-to-life for
armed robbery. The California Adult Authority had reduced
the sentence to four years, fixing an earlier parole date for
two years. After serving the two years, Freddy had been
offered a parole, but he turned it down, preferring to do two
more years and then get out of prison without any strings
attached. He accepted the label in his jacket—the file folder

that held his records in the warden's office—which had him down as a career criminal. He knew that he would commit another crime as soon as he was released, and if he was on parole when he was caught, he would be returned to prison as a parole violator. Violating a parole could mean eight or even ten more years of prison before beginning the new sentence for whatever it was that he was caught doing after he got out.

San Quentin is overcrowded, so there are not enough jobs for everyone and a man must earn a job. Freddy liked to work (when he worked), and he was efficient. Assigned, after several months of idleness, to kitchen duty, he had observed the operation closely. He had then written a ten-page memorandum to the warden, explaining in detail how the staff could be cut and the service improved if certain correction officers and prison chefs were removed and replaced. To Freddy's surprise, he found himself back in the yard.

His report, which would have earned a management major in college a B+, earned Freddy the enmity of several kitchen screws. These officers, with their solid links to the prisoner power structure, directed that Freddy be taught a lesson for his temerity. Two black prisoners cornered Freddy in the yard one afternoon and worked him over. At the yard captain's hearing, they claimed that Freddy had jumped them for no reason and that they were merely attempting to defend themselves from his psychopathic, racist attack. Inasmuch as Freddy had tested out as a psychopath and sociopath (so had the two other prisoners), he was sent to the hole for six days for his unprovoked attack on these innocent inmates. The black yard captain also gave him a short lecture on racism.

During the six dismal days in the hole, which included revocation of Freddy's smoking privileges and reduction to bread and water with a plate of kidney beans every third day, Freddy reviewed his life and realized that altruism had been his major fault.

Back when he had been a juvenile offender, he had been sent to the reform school at Whittier, where he had organized a sit-down strike in the dining hall in an effort to get seconds on Sunday desserts (rice pudding with raisins, of which Freddy was very fond). The campaign failed, and Freddy had stayed at Whittier for the full three years of his sentence.

Again, at Ione, California, in the Preston Institute for Youthful Offenders, Freddy had extended himself, planning the escape of a boy named Enoch Sawyers. Enoch's father, who had caught his son masturbating, had castrated the boy. Mr. Sawyers was a very religious man and considered masturbation a grievous offense to God. Mr. Sawyers was arrested, but because of his religious connections and the laudatory testimony of his minister, he had been sentenced to two years' probation. But when young Enoch, only fifteen years old at the time, had recovered from his unelected surgery, he had become a neighborhood terror. Deprived of his testicles and taunted by his schoolmates, he had demonstrated his manhood almost daily by beating one or more of his tormentors half to death. He was fearless and could take incredible amounts of punishment without, apparently, noticing or caring how badly he was hurt.

Finally, at seventeen, Enoch had been sentenced to Preston as an incorrigible menace to the peace of Fresno, California. At Preston, among some very hardened young prisoners, Enoch again felt compelled to prove his manhood by beating up on people. His technique was to walk up to someone—anyone—and slam a hard right to his fellow prisoner's belly or jaw. He would continue to pummel his victim until the person either fought back or ran away from him.

Enoch's presence in the dormitory was unsettling to the other prisoners. Freddy, to solve the problem, had be-friended him and worked out an escape plan, telling Enoch that he could prove his manhood to the authorities once and for all by escaping. Escaping from Preston was not so difficult, and Enoch, with Freddy's help, got away easily. He was caught in Oakland four days later when he tried to beat up three Chicago beet-pullers and steal their truck. They overpowered him, kicked out his remaining front teeth, and turned him over to the police. Enoch told the officials at Preston that Freddy had planned his escape, so Freddy's good time was revoked. Instead of eighteen months, Freddy spent three years there. Moreover, Freddy had also taken a severe beating as soon as Enoch was returned to Preston.

In the hole at San Quentin, which was not altogether dark—a pale slice of light indicated the bottom of the door—Freddy thought hard about his life. His desire for the good of others had been at the root of his problems, making his own life worse instead of better. And he hadn't really helped anyone else. He decided then to look out only for himself.

He quit smoking. If your smoking privileges are revoked but you don't smoke, the punishment is meaningless. Back in the yard, Freddy had quietly joined the jocks in the daily pumping of iron and had worked on his mind as well as his body. He read *Time* magazine every week and took out a subscription to the *Reader's Digest*. He also gave up sex, trading his pudgy punk, a golden brown Chicano from East Los Angeles, for eight cartons of Chesterfields and 200 Milky Way candy bars. He then traded the Chesterfields (the favorite brand among black prisoners) and 150 of the Milky Ways for a single cell. He also made his peace with the prisoner power structure. He had turned selflessness to self-interest, learning the lesson that everyone must come to eventually: what a man gives up voluntarily cannot be taken away from him.

Now Freddy was out. Because of his good behavior they had let him out after three years instead of making him serve the full four. They needed the space at San Quentin, and inasmuch as some two-thirds of the prisoners were classified as psychopaths, that could not really be held against him. On the day Freddy was released, the assistant warden had advised him not to return to Santa Barbara, but to leave California and find a new state.

"That way," the assistant warden said, "when they catch you again, which they will, it will at least be a first offense in that particular state. And bear in mind, Frenger, you were never very happy here."

The advice had been sound. After three successful muggings in San Francisco—with his powerful muscles, it was a simple matter to twist a man's arm behind his back and ram his head into a wall—Freddy had put three thousand miles between himself and California.

FREDDY TURNED ON the water in the tub and adjusted it for temperature. He undressed and read the information on the placard beside the corridor door. Checkout time was noon, which gave him twenty-four hours. He studied the escape diagram and what to do in case of fire, then took the room service menus into the bathroom. When the tub was filled, he turned off the faucet. He went back to the bar, filled a tall glass with ice and ginger ale, and got into the tub to read the menus.

He glanced at the room service menu, and then studied the wine list. He didn't know one wine from another. Vintage years meant nothing to him, but he was amazed at the prices. The idea of paying a hundred dollars for a bottle of wine, even with a stolen credit card, struck him as outrageous. The thought also made him cautious. He knew that as long as he did not buy anything that cost more than fifty dollars, most clerks would not call the 800 number to check on the status of the credit card. At least this was the usual policy. And in hotels, they usually didn't get around to checking the card until the day you checked out. But he had taken a $135-a-day suite. Well, he wouldn't worry about it, and as he thought about the mugging of Herman T. Gotlieb in the alley, he felt a little more secure. That was the safe thing about mugging gays; the police didn't worry much about what happened to them. At the very least, Mr. Gotlieb had a bad concussion, and he would be a very confused man for some time.

Freddy got out of the tub, dried himself with a gold bath sheet, and wrapped it around his waist. He needed a shave but had nothing to shave with; his face was clean but felt dirty with its blond stubble. He went through his stuffed eelskin wallet again. He had $79 in bills and some loose change. The San Franciscans he had mugged had carried very little folding money. He had seven credit cards, but he was going to need some more cash.

He put the stolen Cardin suitcase on the coffee table. It was locked. If there was a razor in the case he could shave. He didn't have a knife—perhaps there were bar implements. Yes, a corkscrew. It took five minutes to jimmy the two locks. He opened the suitcase and licked his lips. This was always an exciting moment, like opening a surprise package or a grab bag. One never knew what one would find.

It was all women's stuff: nightgowns, skirts, blouses, slippers, and size 6½ shoes in knitted covers. There was a black silk cocktail dress, size seven, a soft blue cashmere sweater, size seven-eight, and a pair of fold-up Cardin sunglasses in a lizard case. The items were all expensive, but there was no razor; apparently, the young mother who had owned the suitcase didn't shave her legs.

Freddy dialed the bell captain and asked to speak with Pablo.

"Pablo," he said, when he got the bellman on the line, "this is Mr. Gotlieb up in seven-seventeen."

"Yes, sir."

"I'd like a girl sent up. A fairly small one, size seven or eight."

"How tall?"

"I'm not sure. How tall are sevens and eights?"

"They can run pretty tall, from five feet on up to maybe five-six or more."

"That doesn't make any sense. How could one dress fit a woman five feet tall or five feet, six inches tall?"

"I don't know, Mr. Gotlieb, but women's sizes run funny. My wife wears a size twenty-two hat. I wear a seven and a quarter, and my head's a lot bigger than hers."

"All right. Just send me up a small one."

"For how long?"

"I don't know. What difference does it make?"

"You're still on nooner rates. I've got one small one for you now, but she gets off at five. That's all I got now. Tonight, I can get you another one, even smaller."

"No. That's okay. I won't even need her till five."

"In about twenty minutes, then?"

"Tell her to bring me up a club sandwich, with some dill pickle slices on the side."

"She can't do that, sir, but I'll send the room service waiter up with the club sandwich."

"Good. And I'll take care of you later."

"Yes, sir."

The club sandwich, a nice one with white turkey meat, bacon, American cheese, lettuce, and tomato slices on white toast, was $12, plus a $1 service charge. Freddy signed for it and gave the waiter a $1 tip. Even though there were pickles, potato chips, cole slaw, and extra paper cups of mayonnaise and mustard on the side, Freddy was appalled by the price of the club sandwich. What in the hell had happened to the economy while he was in prison?

Freddy ate half the sandwich and all of the pickle slices, then put the other half into the refrigerator. The other half, he thought, is worth six bucks—Jesus!

There was a light knock on the door. Freddy unfastened the chain and opened the door, and a young girl with small and very even teeth came in. She was a small one, all right, standing about five-three in her high heels. Her well-defined widow's peak and smallish chin made her face heart-shaped. She wore tight jeans with ROLLS-ROYCE embroidered on the left leg in three-inch white block letters; a

U-neck purple T-shirt, and dangling gold earrings. Her soft kangaroo leather drawstring bag was big enough to hold schoolbooks. Freddy estimated her age at fifteen—maybe sixteen.

"Mr. Gotlieb?" she said, smiling, "Pablo said you wanted to talk to me."

"Yeah," Freddy said. "How old are you, anyway?"

"Nineteen. My name is Pepper."

"Yeah. Sure it is. You got any ID?"

"My driver's license. I just look young because I don't wear makeup, that's all."

"Let's see the license."

"I don't have to show it to you."

"That's right. You don't. You can leave."

"But if I show it to you, you'll know my right name."

"But I'll still call you Pepper."

She took her wallet out of the bag and showed Freddy her Florida license. The name on the license was Susan Waggoner, and she was twenty years old—not nineteen.

"This says you're twenty."

She shrugged. "I like being a teenager."

"What're the rates?"

"For nooners—half-hour limit—fifty dollars until five o'clock. Then it goes up to seventy-five. I get off at five, so for you it's only fifty, unless you want extras."

"Okay. Let's go into the bedroom."

Pepper pulled down the spread on the queen-size bed, then the sheets, and smoothed them out. She slipped off her shoes, her T-shirt, and her jeans. She was not wearing a bra, nor did she need one. She rolled off her panties, lay down on the bed, and put her hands behind her head as she spread her skinny legs. As she locked her fingers behind her head, her small breasts almost disappeared, except for the taut strawberry nipples. Her long auburn hair, in a ponytail fastened with a rubber band, made a curling question mark on the right side of the pillow. Her well-greased pubic hair was a kinky brownish yellow.

Freddy unwrapped the bath sheet and dropped it on the floor. He probed her pregreased vagina with the first three fingers of his right hand. He shook his head and frowned.

"Not enough friction there for me," he said. "I'm used to boys, you see. Do you take it in the ass?"

"No, sir. I should, I know, but I tried it once and it hurt too much. I just can't do it. I can give you a blow job if you like."

"That's okay, but I'm not all that interested anyway. You really should learn to take it in the ass. You'll make more money, and if you learn how to relax—"

"That's what Pablo said, but I just can't."

"What size dress do you wear?"

"It depends. I can wear a five sometimes, but usually I'm either a six or a seven. It depends on who makes it. They all have different sizes."

"Try this on." Freddy brought her the black silk dress from the sitting room. "Put your shoes on first, and then look at the mirror. There's a full-length mirror on the back of the bathroom door."

Pepper slipped into the dress, turned sideways as she looked into the mirror, and smiled. "It looks nice on me, doesn't it? I'd have to take it in some at the waist though."

"You can have it for fifty bucks."

"All I've got with me's a twenty. I'll give you a free blow job for it."

"That's no offer! A man can get a free blow job anywhere. The hell with it. I'm not a salesman. Keep the dress. And while you're here, take this suitcase full of stuff. There're some skirts and other things in it, and a nice cashmere sweater. Take the suitcase too."

"Where'd you get all these nice clothes?"

"They belong to my wife. When I left my wife I took the stuff with me. I paid for it, so it was mine to take."

"You left your wife?"

"Yeah. We're getting a divorce."

"Because of the boys?"

"What boys?"

"You said you were used to boys, and I just assumed that—"

"Jesus Christ. How long've you been working for Pablo?"

"Since the beginning of the semester. I go to Miami-Dade Community College, Downtown. I need the money for school."

"Well, one of the first things you should learn is not to ask clients personal questions."

"I'm sorry. I didn't mean to pry." She started to cry.

"Why're you crying, for Christ's sake?"

"I don't know. I just do sometimes. I'm not doing very good at this, not even nooners, and when I go back to Pablo without any money, he'll—"

"There's a plastic laundry bag in the closet. Put the clothes in it, and give Pablo the empty suitcase. He can get the locks fixed, and he'll have a two-hundred-dollar suitcase. I'll square you with Pablo later. Okay?"

Pepper stopped crying, wiped her eyes, and got back into her own clothes. She packed the clothing neatly into the plastic laundry bag.

"What do you do when you get off duty at five?"

"I usually walk downtown, have some dinner, and then go to class. Tonight's my English class at six-fifteen, and it runs until seven-forty, unless Mr. Turner lets us out early. Sometimes, when we've got a paper to write, he lets us go home to write it."

Why, Freddy wondered, is she lying to me? No college would ever accept this incredibly stupid young woman as a student. On the other hand, he had known a few college men in San Quentin. Although they usually got the best jobs there, they didn't appear to be any smarter than the majority of the cons. Maybe the girl wasn't lying. He didn't know anything about college requirements, but maybe they would be much lower for women than for men. It would be a good idea to have a woman with a car show him the city. So far it was all white buildings and a blur of greenery.

"I'll tell you what, Pepper. I'll buy you dinner and then wait for you to get out of class. Then you can drive me around some. You've got a license, so I suppose you've got a car?"

"My brother's car. I get to keep it all the time, but I've got to meet him at the airport at eight-thirty tonight to collect some money from him. He works out there, and gives me his pay every day to deposit in the bank. Where he works, he isn't allowed to have a car."

"You don't live together?"

"Not anymore. We did at first, when we first came down to Miami from Okeechobee, but now I've got the apartment to myself."

"That's all right. I don't mind riding out to the airport again. I just want to get familiar with the city. I'll give you a decent tip, or buy you a drink, or maybe take you to a movie. What do you say?"

She smiled. "I'd like that. I haven't had a *date* date since I came down here, Mr. Gotlieb—"

"You can call me Junior."

"Junior? All right, and you can call me Susie. Pablo told me to call myself Pepper so that customers would think I was hot. Pablo's my manager, like, and he knows all about these things. Most men, I've noticed, just laugh when I tell them my name is Pepper. You didn't—Junior—and I think you're awfully nice."

"I am nice, Susie, and I like you a lot. I'll tell you what. Just leave the bag of clothes with me and take the suitcase down to Pablo. That way he won't know you got the stuff, and I can take it with me when we meet."

"I usually eat dinner at Granny's. It's a health food restaurant right near the campus, about eight blocks from here. I walk because I leave the car in the parking garage near the school, but you can take a cab there. The cabbies all know where it is, even the ones who don't speak English."

She handed him the bag of clothing.

"I'll see you at Granny's at five, then."

"It'll be closer to five-fifteen, but I'll get there as soon as I can."

"Good. And have a prosperous afternoon."

"Thank you. But whatever you do, don't tell Pablo. We aren't supposed to go out with the johns—that's why I want you to meet me at Granny's."

"Pablo, in my opinion, is an asshole. I'll just tell him I had jet lag and that kept me from performing. I'll slip him ten bucks and he'll be so happy he won't say a word to you. But I won't tell him about our date. Don't worry."

Susan blushed, and looked shyly at the floor. "You can kiss me on the cheek and sorta seal our date. That way I know you'll really come to Granny's. I know you men don't like to kiss us on the mouth . . ."

"I don't mind kissing you on the mouth."

"You don't?"

Freddy kissed her chastely, almost tenderly, on the lips, and then led her to the door. She waggled her fingers and smiled; then he closed the door after her and chain-locked it. She had forgotten the empty suitcase, and he still had the bag of clothes. He would give the suitcase to Pablo instead of the ten bucks he had intended to give him. As long as he had the clothes, he knew she would come to Granny's.

He still had plenty of time to do some shopping.

4

BILL HENDERSON AND Hoke Moseley worked on their reports for the rest of the afternoon at the double desk they shared in a glass-walled cubbyhole at the new Miami Police Station. As sergeants they were entitled to the tiny office, which had a door that could be closed and locked, but it was much more crowded and uncomfortable than the space the other plainclothes detectives had in the large, outer bullpen. The room was undecorated, except for a twenty-two-by-thirty-inch poster on the one unglassed wall. A hand holding a pistol, with the pistol aimed at the viewer, was in the center of the wall. The message, in bold black letters beneath the pointing pistol, read MIAMI—SEE IT LIKE A NATIVE.

When they took the depositions of the brothers Peeples, only one man at a time could be accommodated in the tiny room. Irritated by the Georgians' uncooperative attitudes, they let the two men find their own way back to the airport by taxi instead of returning them to the PR man in a police car.

Hoke flipped a quarter. Henderson lost, which meant that Henderson had to call Martin Waggoner's father in Okeechobee and break the sad news. While Henderson called,

Hoke went downstairs to the station cafeteria and got two cups of coffee in Styrofoam cups. He drank his in the cafeteria and brought the other cup, now barely warm, back upstairs to Henderson. Henderson took one sip of the lukewarm coffee, replaced the lid, and dropped the cup into the wastebasket.

"Mr. Waggoner said his son had a sister living with him here in Miami, and he wouldn't accept the truth of his son's death until she identified the body. His son was a deeply religious boy, he claimed, and was not the kind to fight anyone. I told him there wasn't any fight, and about how it happened and all, and he said that there had to be more to it than that. I know how he feels, the poor bastard. When I told him his son died from a broken finger I felt like I was lying myself."

"He didn't die from a broken finger. He died from shock."

Henderson shrugged. "I know. And I told him what Doc Evans said about shock. Anyway, I made the call to Mr. Waggoner, so you can take the sister down to identify the body."

"You lost the coin toss—"

"And I called Mr. Waggoner. The sister's a new development, and my wife expects me home for dinner. We're having company over. You're single—"

"Divorced."

"But single, with no responsibilities or obligations."

"I pay alimony and child support for two teenage daughters."

"Sometimes you break my heart. Your evenings are bleak and empty. You have no friends—"

"I thought you and I were friends?"

"We are. That's why you can get a hold of the sister while I go home to my assertive wife, my gawky teenager son, and my daughter with acne. I can then entertain for drinks and dinner a couple my wife likes and I can't stand."

"Okay, since you point out the joys I'm missing, I'll go. Got her address?"

"I wrote it all down, and I've made some calls. She lives in Kendall Pines Terrace out on One-fifty-seventh Avenue. Building Six-East, apartment four-one-eight."

"Kendall? That's a helluva ways out." Hoke transferred the information from the yellow pad to his notebook.

"Luckily for you she isn't home. Susan Waggoner goes to Miami-Dade, to the New World Campus downtown. She'll be in class at six-fifteen. I already called the registrar, so if you stop by the office, they'll send a student assistant up to the classroom with you and get the girl out of class. You've even got time to get a drink first. Two drinks."

"And so everything works out for the best, doesn't it? You can go home to dinner, and I can escort a hysterical young girl to the morgue to see her dead brother. I can, then, in all probability, drive her to hell and gone out to Kendall and get her calmed down. Then I have to drive her all the way back to Miami Beach. Maybe, if I'm lucky, I'll be home in time to watch the eleven o'clock news."

"What the hell, Hoke, it's all overtime pay."

"Compensatory time. I've used up my overtime pay this month."

"What's the difference?"

"Twenty-five bucks. Haven't we had this conversation before?"

"Last month. Only last month it was me who had to sit in the hardware store until four A.M. while you went home to bed."

"But you were on overtime pay."

"Compensatory time."

"What's the difference?"

"Twenty-five bucks."

They both laughed, but laughing didn't mask Hoke's uneasiness. He didn't know which was worse—telling a father that his son was dead or telling a sister that her brother was dead, but he was glad he didn't have to tell both of them.

5

IN HIS NEW clothes Freddy looked like a native Miamian. He wore a pale blue *guayabera,* white linen slacks with tiny golden tennis rackets embroidered at irregular intervals on both pants legs, white patent-leather loafers with tassels, a chromium dolphin-shaped belt buckle, and pale blue socks that matched his guayabera. He had had a $20 haircut and an $8 shave in the hotel barber shop, charging both to his room, together with a generous tip for the barber. He could have passed as a local, or as a tourist down from Pennsylvania to spend the full season.

Freddy arrived at Granny's a little before five and ordered a pot of ginseng tea, telling the heavy-hipped Cuban waitress that he was waiting for a friend. He had never tasted ginseng tea before, but he managed to kill some of the bitterness by adding three spoons of raw brown sugar to his cup. The menu didn't make much sense to Freddy. After looking it over, he decided he would order whatever Susan ordered and hope for the best. The ginseng tea was foul, but it had seemed like a better choice than the gunpowder tea the waitress had recommended. He had run out of cigarettes, his first pack smoked since leaving prison. But when he asked the waitress to bring him a fresh package of

28

Winston 100s, she told him that no smoking was allowed at Granny's, and that "cigarettes are poison to the body."

Actually, Freddy realized, he didn't truly want a cigarette. Kicking the habit in prison had been difficult. Six days in the hole without a cigarette had given him a good start, helping his body get rid of the stored nicotine, but it hadn't helped his psychological dependence on smoking. There were very few things that a man could do alone in prison. Smoking was one of them. Smoking not only helped to pass the time, it gave a man something to do with his hands. Until he started pumping iron in earnest, those long days of wandering around in the yard without a cigarette had been his worst days in stir. And yet the first thing he had done when he got into the San Francisco bus terminal was to buy a package of Winston 100s. He had picked them because of the deep red package. He had somehow associated smoking with freedom, even though smoking was a form of slavery. That settled it. He would give it up before he got back into the habit. Otherwise, when he got back to prison, he would have to go through all of that painful withdrawal business again.

Susan, still in her work clothes, arrived a few minutes after five. She waved from the door and then joined him at the table-for-two against the wall. She ducked her head and sat under an ominous hanging basket containing a drooping mass of ferns. She was obviously pleased to see Freddy.

"You forgot the suitcase," Freddy said, "but I gave it to Pablo. The clothes are in the bag under the table."

"I didn't really forget. I just thought better of it. A lot of employees know what I do in the hotel, and they don't like me. They don't like any of us girls, because of the money we make. So if a maid saw me with a suitcase, she'd call the security office and say that I stole it from a guest or something. Then, when I told the security officer the truth, he'd still check with you, and he'd find out that you didn't have any other luggage. That could make some trouble for you. What I think, when you left your wife, is that you took

29

the wrong suitcase. You took hers instead of your own. Isn't that right?"

"Something like that. That's interesting, Susan. I didn't think you could figure out something that complicated."

"I wasn't always a thoughtful person. When I was in high school in Okeechobee, all I thought about was having a good time. But at Miami-Dade, the teachers want us to use our minds."

"Where's Okeechobee?"

"It's up by the lake, when you drive north to Disney World."

"What lake?"

"Lake Okeechobee!" Susan laughed. "It's the biggest lake in the whole South. Everybody gets their water down here from Lake Okeechobee."

"I'm from California. I don't know shit about Florida."

"I don't know shit about California, either. So I guess we're even."

"Lake Tahoe's a pretty good-size lake in California. Have you heard of Tahoe?"

"I've heard of it, but I don't know where it is."

"Part of it's in Nevada, and the rest is in California. On the Nevada side, you can gamble in the casinos."

"You can't gamble in Florida, except on horses, race track and trotters, on dogs, and jai alai. Oh, yes, you can gamble on cockfighting and dogfighting, too, if you know where to go. But all other form of gambling, the governor says, are immoral."

"Is the governor a Jesuit?"

"That's a Catholic, isn't it?"

"An educated Catholic, the way it was explained to me."

"No, he's a Protestant. It would be a waste of money for a Catholic to run for office down here."

"Tell me about Okeechobee, and tell me why you came to Miami."

"It's a lot hotter up there than it is here, for one thing. And it rains more, too, because of the lake. It's a little town, not big like Miami, but there's lots to do, like bowling and going juking, or fishing and swimming. If you don't like country, you wouldn't like Okeechobee. If a girl doesn't get married, there isn't much future there, and nobody ever asked me to get married. I did the cooking for my daddy and my brother, but that didn't stop me from getting pregnant. That's why I came to Miami, really, to get me an abortion. My father said it was a disgrace to get pregnant that way, and he told me not to come back—"

"The *Reader's Digest* said about forty percent of the girls who get pregnant aren't married. What's he so uptight about?"

"My brother, Marty, had a big fight with him about that. He told daddy it's the Lord's right to punish people, and that daddy didn't have any right to sit in judgment on me. So the upshot of all that was that Marty had to go with me, and he was told not to come back either. Daddy doesn't believe in much of anything, and Marty's really religious, you see."

"So you both came down to Miami?"

She nodded. "On the bus. Marty and me are really close. We were born only ten months apart, and he's always taken my side against daddy."

The waitress interrupted. "You want more tea, or d'you want to order now?"

"I'll have the Circe Salad," Susan said. "I always get that."

"Me, too," Freddy said.

"You'll like the Circe Salad. Daddy gets mad, but he always gets over it. I think we could go back now, and he wouldn't say a word. But we've done so well down here, we're going to stay a long time. We're saving our money, and when we've got enough saved Marty wants to go back to Okeechobee and get us a Burger King franchise. He'll be the day manager, and I'll manage nights. We'll build a house on the lake, get us a speedboat, and everything."

"Marty has it all figured out."

Susan nodded. "That's why I'm going to Miami-Dade.

When I finish English and social science, I'm going to take business and management courses."

"What about your mother? What does she think about you two leaving?"

"I don't know where she is, and neither does daddy. She was working the counter at the truck stop, and then one night, when I was only five, she ran off with a truck driver. Daddy traced her as far as New Orleans, paying a private detective, and then the trail got cold.

"But Marty and me are doing real good here. He's got a job collecting money for the Hare Krishnas, and he gives at least a hundred dollars of it every day to me to put in the bank. It's a hard life for Marty, compared to mine, because he's restricted to camp at night, and he has to get up at four A.M. every morning to pray. But he doesn't mind working seven days a week at the airport, not when he makes a hundred dollars a day for us to save."

"I think I saw one out at the airport today. I don't understand this Hare Krishna business. What are they, anyway? It doesn't sound American."

"They are now. It's some kind of religious cult from India, a professional beggars' group, and now they're all over the United States. They must be in California, too."

"Maybe so. I never heard of them before, that's all."

"Well, Marty saw the advantages right away, because it's a way to beg legally."

Susan leaned forward and lowered her voice.

"What he does, you see, is put a dollar in one pocket for the Krishnas, and a dollar in another pocket for us. The Krishnas, being a religious organization, can beg at airports, whereas if you were to go out there and beg, they'd put you in jail."

"In other words, your brother's stealing the Krishnas blind."

"I guess you can put it that way. He said they'd kick him out if they ever found out. But they aren't going to catch on. I meet Marty every night by the mailbox outside the Airport

Hotel, which is right inside the airport. While I pretend to mail a letter, he slips the money into my purse. He's got a partner who's supposed to be watching him, but Marty can always get away for a minute to go to the men's room. What I can't understand is why those passengers out there hand him fives and tens, and sometimes a twenty, just because he asks for it. He says they're afraid not to, that they're all guilty about something they've done bad. But he sure collects a lot of money on a twelve-hour shift out there."

The waitress brought their Circe Salads: large chunks of romaine lettuce, orange slices, bean and wheat sprouts, shredded coconut, a blob of vanilla yogurt, and a topping of grated sugar-cane sawdust soaked in ginseng. The salad was served in a porcelain bowl in the shape of a giant clam shell.

"I've never eaten in a health food restaurant before."

"Me neither, till I came to Miami. You don't have to eat it if you don't like it."

"I don't like the ginseng root. Do they put it in everything here?"

"Just about. It's supposed to make you feel sexy, so they use ginseng because they don't serve meat here. That's the reason, I think."

"I'd rather have meat. This would be all right without the ginseng taste. How'd you do this afternoon?"

"Fifty dollars. One Colombian, and an old man from Dayton, Ohio. Counting all those clothes you gave me, it was a good day for me. Besides, I got to meet you. You're the nicest man I've ever met."

"I think you're nice, too."

"Your hands are just beautiful."

"Nobody ever told me that before. Here—take the rest of my salad."

"You didn't even try the yogurt."

"Yogurt? I thought it was soured ice cream."

"No, it's yogurt. It's supposed to taste a little sour."

"I don't like it."

"I'm sorry, Junior. I guess I should've had you meet me at the Burger King. It's right across from the school."

"I'm not hungry. I had a club sandwich in my room, before I bought these new clothes."

"Your blue shirt matches your eyes. Did you buy it because it matched your eyes?"

"No. I liked the extra pockets. It's too hot to wear a jacket, and I need the pockets. Is it always this hot?"

"It's only about eighty-five. That's normal for October. In the summer it gets really hot, especially up in Okeechobee. And then there's mosquitoes, too. It gets so hot you can't do anything even if you wanted to. When you go out to a drive-in movie at night, all you do is sweat and drink beer and spray Cutter's."

"Cutter's?"

"That's mosquito spray, and it really works, too. Oh, they'll still buzz around your ears, but they won't land on you—not if you spray on enough Cutter's. There's another brand, when you spray too much on, you get a rash. But you don't care about the rash, because you've already got a rash from prickly heat. We better pay and go to class."

"I'll pay. Give me the ticket."

"No, it's my treat. If you want to, you can go to class with me. It's air-conditioned, and Professor Turner won't mind. He'll think you're a member of the class anyway. He told us he doesn't learn our names. He finds out the names of the A and F students soon enough, he says, and the rest of us don't matter. I'm only a C student in English, so he's never even called on me yet."

THERE WERE THIRTY-FIVE students in the class; thirty-six, counting Freddy, who took the last seat in the row by the back wall, behind Susan. There were no windows, and the walls, except for the green blackboard, were covered with cork. The city noises were shut out completely. The students, mostly Latinos and blacks, were silent as they watched the teacher write *Haiku* on the green board with a piece of orange chalk. The teacher, a heavy-set and bearded man in his late forties, did not take roll; he had just waited for silence before writing on the board.

"Haiku," he said, in a well-trained voice, "is a seventeen-syllable poem that the Japanese have been writing for several centuries. I don't speak Japanese, but as I understand haiku, pronounced *ha—ee—koo,* much of the beauty is lost in the translation from Japanese to English.

"English isn't a good language for rhymes. Three-quarters of the poetry written in English is unrhymed because of the paucity of rhyming words. Unhappily for you Spanish-speaking students, you have so many words ending in vowels, you have the difficulty in reverse.

"At any rate, here is a haiku in English."

He wrote on the board:

> *The Miami sun,*
> *Rising in the Everglades—*
> *Burger in a bun.*

"This haiku," he continued, "which I made up in Johnny Raffa's bar before I came to class, is a truly rotten poem. But I assure you I had no help with it. Basho, the great Japanese poet, if he knew English and if he were still alive, would positively detest it. But he would recognize it as a haiku because it has five syllables in the first line, seven in the second, and five in the third. Add them up and you have seventeen syllables, all you need for a haiku, and all of them concentrating on a penetrating idea.

"You're probably thinking, those of you who wonder about things like this, why am I talking about Japanese poetry? I'll tell you. I want you to write simple sentences— subject, verb, object. I want you to use concrete words that convey exact meanings.

"I know you Spanish-speaking students don't know many Anglo-Saxon words, but that's because you persist in speaking Spanish to one another outside of class instead of

35

practicing English. Except for giving you Fs on your papers, I can't help you much there. But when you write your papers, pore—*p-o-r-e*—over your dictionaries for concrete words. When you write in English, force your reader to reach for something."

There was a snicker at the back of the room.

"Basho wrote haikus in the seventeenth century, and they're still being read and talked about in Japan today. There are a couple of hundred haiku magazines in Japan, and every month articles are still being written about Basho's most famous haiku. I'll give you the literal translation instead of a seventeen-syllable translation."

He wrote on the blackboard:

> *Old pond.*
> *Frog jumps in.*
> *Water sound.*

"There you have it," Mr. Turner said, scratching his beard with the piece of chalk. "Old pond. Frog jumps in. Water sound. What's missing, of course, is the onomatopoeia of the water sound. But the meaning is clear enough. What does it mean?"

He looked around the room but was unsuccessful in catching anyone's eye. The students, with sullen mouths and lowered lids, studied books and papers on their armrest desk tops.

"I can wait," Mr. Turner said. "You know me well enough by now to know that I can wait for a volunteer for about fifteen minutes before my patience runs out. I wish I could wait longer, because while I'm waiting for volunteers I don't have to teach." He folded his arms.

A young man wearing cut-off jeans, a faded blue tank top, and scuffed running shoes without socks, lifted his right hand two inches above his desk top.

"You, then," the teacher said, pointing with his chalk.

"What it means, I think," the student began, "is that

36

there's an old pond of water. This frog, wanting to get into the water, comes along and jumps in. When he plops into the water he makes a sound, like splash."

"Very good! That's about as literal an interpretation as you can get. But if that's all there is to the poem, why would serious young men in Japan write papers about this poem every month in their haiku magazines? But, thank you. At least we have the literal translation out of the way.

"Now, let's say that Miami represents the old pond. You, or most of you, anyway, came here from somewhere else. You come to Miami, that is, and you jump into this old pond. We've got a million and a half people here already, so the splash you make isn't going to make a very large sound. Or is it? It surely depends upon the frog. Some of you, I'm afraid, will make a very large splash, and we'll all hear it. Some will make a splash so faint that it won't be heard by your next door neighbor. But at least we're all in the same pond, and—"

There was a knock on the door. Annoyed, Mr. Turner crossed to the door and opened it. Freddy leaned forward and whispered to Susan. "That's some pretty heavy shit he's laying down. D'you know what he's talking about?"

Susan shook her head.

"Us! You, your brother, and me. What's the other word mean he keeps talking about—*onomatopoeia?*"

"It's the word for the actual sound. Like *splash*, when the frog jumps in."

"Right! See what I mean?" Freddy's eyes glittered. "You and me, Susan. We're going to make us a big splash in this town."

6

PROFESSOR TURNER STEPPED back into the room and cleared his throat. "Is Susan Waggoner here today?"

She raised her hand.

"Come out into the hallway, please. Bring your things with you."

Susan put her books into her oversize bag. Freddy followed her into the corridor, carrying the laundry bag. The teacher frowned at Freddy and shook his head.

"This doesn't concern you, son. Go back to your seat."

"If it concerns Susan it concerns me," Freddy said. "We're engaged."

Sergeant Hoke Moseley, looking at the floor, lifted his head and nodded when the student assistant asked him if she could leave.

"Susan," Mr. Turner said, "do what you've got to do, and stay out of school as long as it takes. When you return to class, see me in my office and I'll let you make up any assignments you missed." He looked sternly at Freddy for a long moment. "You've already missed several classes, but the same goes for you." He returned to his classroom and closed the door.

Hoke showed the pair his shield. "Sergeant Moseley.

Homicide. Isn't there a lounge somewhere where we can sit down and talk?" Hoke hadn't expected to see such a young girl. She looked more like a high school kid than a college student. But if she was engaged to this hard-looking jock, she was probably older than she looked. It was a help to have the fiancé present; maybe he wouldn't have to drive her out to hell-and-gone Kendall after all. Her boyfriend could take her home.

"There's a student lounge down on the second floor," Susan said. "We can go there. I haven't done anything bad. Have I, Junior?"

Hoke smiled. "Of course you haven't." Hoke started toward the elevator. "Let's go down to the lounge."

They sat at a glass-topped table on three unstable wire Eames chairs in the study area near the Down escalator to the main floor. Hoke lit a cigarette and held out the package. When they shook their heads, he took one drag and dropped the cigarette into an empty Coke can on the table.

"I've got some bad news for you, Miss Waggoner. That's why I wanted you to be seated. Your brother, Martin, in a freaky accident at the airport, died today. And your father, when we called him in Okeechobee, asked us to have you identify the body. We've got an ID already from the other man who was working with your brother at the airport, so there's no mistake. It's just that we need a relative for a positive identification. After the autopsy we can turn the body over to either you or your father. You are eighteen, aren't you?"

"Nineteen," Susan said.

"Twenty," Freddy amended.

"Just barely twenty. This is hard to believe. How did it happen?"

"An unidentified assailant broke your brother's finger, and Martin went into immediate shock and died from this unexpected trauma to his middle digit." Hoke pursed his lips. "It happens sometimes."

"I've changed my mind, officer," Freddy said. "Can I borrow one of your cigarettes?"

"Sure." Hoke offered the pack, and held a match for Freddy to light the cigarette.

Susan shook her head, looking bewildered. "The airport's a dangerous place to work. My brother's been attacked out there before, you know. A man in the men's room gave him a black eye once, and a lady from Cincinnati kneed him in the balls one morning. He walked bowlegged for almost three days. He reported both cases to the security people out there and they just laughed."

"I'm not surprised," Hoke said. "Your brother was a Krishna, and the airport lost its case in court when they tried to get them barred from begging out there. So I can see how security would turn their heads the other way when Krishnas are attacked. On the other hand, the Krishnas annoy a lot of people with their aggressive tactics."

"What do you think, Junior?" Susan turned her head.

Freddy dropped his cigarette into the Coke can. "I think we should go and take a look at the body right now. It may not be Marty after all, and I'm pretty sure the sergeant here would like to get it over with and go home to his dinner."

"My car's down in the patio." Hoke started for the escalator, and they followed him.

Hoke's well-battered 1974 Le Mans was indeed parked on the school patio. He had been unable to find a parking place on the street, so he had jumped the curb and driven over the flagstones to within a few yards of the escalator. There were winos lounging on the patio benches. Two old men, by the wall outside the bookstore, slept noisily on flattened cardboard boxes. Two other derelicts on a nearby concrete bench jeered and gave Hoke the finger as he unlocked the alarm in the left front fender and then unlocked the door and took his police placard off the dashboard. He shoved the placard under the front seat before unlocking the door to the passenger side of the car.

"We'd better all sit in front," Hoke suggested. "A man

40

was sick on the back seat yesterday, and I haven't had a chance to get it cleaned up yet."

Susan sat in the middle. Freddy, on the outside, unrolled his window. "Why does the college let these winos hang around the school?" Freddy said.

"They suspended the old vagrancy laws a few years back. We can't arrest 'em anymore, and if we could, where would we put 'em? On top of the normal eight thousand vags who come down here for the winter, we've got another twenty thousand Nicaraguans, ten thousand Haitian refugees, and another twenty-five thousand Marielitos running around town."

"What's a Marielito?" Freddy said.

"Where have you been?" Hoke said, not unkindly. "Our wimpy ex-president, Jimmy Carter, opened his arms to one hundred and twenty-five thousand Cubans back in 1980. Most of them were legitimate, with families already here in Miami, but Castro also opened his prisons and insane asylums and sent along another twenty-five thousand hardcore criminals, gays, and maniacs. They sailed here from Mariel, in Cuba, so they call them Marielitos."

As Hoke reached forward and switched off the police calls on his radio, a ragged Latin man came up to his window and pounded on it with his fists, shouting:

"Gimme money! Gimme money!"

"See what I mean?" Hoke said. "When you drive around Miami, Susan, always keep your windows rolled up. Otherwise, they'll reach in and steal your purse."

"I know," Susan said, "my brother told me."

Hoke backed expertly into the street, honking his horn until the traffic gave way.

As Hoke drove north on Biscayne Boulevard toward the city morgue, Freddy said, "This old boat rides pretty smooth. You wouldn't think so, just from looking at it."

"I had a new engine put in it. It's my own car, not a police vehicle. The radio belongs to the department, and the red light, but they give us detectives mileage if we use our own personal vehicles. Fifteen cents a mile, which doesn't begin to cover it, and nothing for amortization. But the convenience is worth it. If you order a vehicle from the motor pool you have to wait for a half-hour or more, and then it may be low on gas or have a bad tire or something. So I usually drive my own car. I should do something about the dents, but I'd have them back again the next day. Twenty percent of the drivers in Miami can't qualify for a license, so they drive without one."

The morgue was a low one-story building. Its limited storage space had been supplemented by two leased air-conditioned trailers to keep up with the flow of bodies that were delivered every day. Hoke parked, and they followed him into the office. Dr. Evans had left for the day, but Dr. Ramirez, an assistant pathologist, took them to a gurney in the hallway and showed them the body.

"That's Martin, all right," Susan said quietly.

"I never met Martin, sergeant, but he looks like a nice guy," Freddy said. "He doesn't look anything like you, Susan."

"Not now he doesn't, but back when we were little and almost the same size, people used to take us for fraternal twins." She looked up at Hoke. "We were born only ten months apart, although Marty looks older than me now." Tears welled from Susan's eyes, and she brushed them away impatiently.

"Is it true," Freddy asked Hoke, "that a man's hair and fingernails keep growing after he's dead? I notice some stubble there on Marty's chin."

"I don't know, although I've heard that myself. Is it true, Dr. Ramirez?"

"No, it isn't true. That's just normal stubble on his face. He probably shaved this morning, and that's just his growth for today. One thing for sure, the nail on his middle finger won't grow any longer. The finger was broke clean off. We haven't done the autopsy yet, but Pussgut took a cursory look when he first came in, and there were no other wounds."

" 'Pussgut,' " Hoke explained to Freddy and Susan, "is what the people around here call Dr. Evans when he isn't around to hear them say it. They call him that because of his paunch."

"I'm sorry," Dr. Ramirez said. "I meant to say 'Dr. Evans.' Is the sister here going to sign the papers?"

"I'll sign something to say he's my brother, but I won't sign anything else. Anything else, funeral arrangements or anything, you'll have to notify my father. It's his responsibility, not mine."

In the office, Susan signed the form Dr. Ramirez made out. He Xeroxed a copy on the office machine and gave it to Hoke. Hoke folded the Xeroxed form into a square and tucked it into his notebook. They shook hands with Dr. Ramirez and then went out to the car. When they were seated, Hoke suggested that they stop for a drink.

"Fine with me," Freddy said. "But make it some place where I can get a sandwich."

"We'll stop at a Brazilian steak house on Biscayne. They've got the best steak sandwiches in town."

They were shown to a table right away. Hoke ordered a rum and Coke, Freddy a glass of red wine, and Susan asked for a Shirley Temple, claiming she never drank anything stronger than beer and that she didn't feel like having a beer on top of the yogurt she had eaten for dinner. The waiter, a Salvadoran with very little English, had difficulty with the Shirley Temple. Hoke had to cross over to the bar and explain to the Costa Rican bartender how to make it.

Hoke waved away the menu, which was printed in Portuguese, and ordered two steak sandwiches and three flans. The steak sandwiches arrived, redolent of garlic, along with the desserts.

Freddy dug into the custard immediately, and finished it before he covered his sandwich with A-1 Sauce.

"Where'd you do your time?" Hoke asked Freddy. "Marianna or Raiford?"

"Time? What time? What makes you think I did time?"

Hoke shrugged. "The way you tucked into that flan, and because you ate it first, before tackling your sandwich. How long were you in Marianna?"

"I don't even know where Marianna is."

"It's our state juvenile reform school. Where're you from?"

"California. Santa Barbara. I came here to Miami to study management at Miami-Dade. When we graduate, me and Susan're going to get us a Burger King franchise somewhere. So she's studying business and management, too. I think I see what you mean, though, about eating my dessert first. But that's because I was an orphan and raised in a foster home. There were three other guys there, all of us about the same age, and you more or less had to eat your dessert first or somebody else would snatch it."

"The same ritual, you'll discover, is practiced at Raiford. So at least if you ever get into trouble down here you've got a good habit going for you. I didn't get your name, except for the 'Junior.'"

"Ramon Mendez."

"You don't have a Spanish accent. Have you got your green card?"

"I'm not a Chicano, I'm an American citizen. And I've got ID if you want to see it. Just because a man's got a Spanish name, that doesn't make him a refugee or something. It just so happens that Mendez was my father's name, but my mother was as big a WASP as you are. Besides, I already told you I was brought up with all white guys in a foster home!"

"Don't get excited, Ramon. We're just having a little pleasant conversation here. Do you speak Spanish?"

"A little, sure. I went to school in Santa Barbara, and we had our share of Chicanos out there. You pick it up a little

44

playing softball. You know, shouting 'Arriba, arriba!' when a guy's trying to reach second base on a steal."

"You pump a little iron, too, right?"

"A little. I can jerk three-twenty-five, but I don't like to do it. I'm not really into heavy lifting. I just like to work out, that's all."

"What's your bicep?"

Freddy shrugged. "I haven't measured in a while. It used to be twenty-one inches. I doubt if it's that much now."

"I'm impressed."

"Well, I'm not one of your body lovers. As I said, I just like to work out for the exercise, that's all."

Hoke turned to Susan. "How's your Shirley Temple, Miss Waggoner? Would you rather have some coffee? Some espresso?"

"No, no, this is fine. I was supposed to meet my brother at the airport tonight at eight-thirty. And he was gonna give me two hundred dollars to make the car payment. D'you have his wallet and money for me?"

"If you phone your father and ask him to call me and okay it, I can hand over the effects. There's a little more than two hundred in the wallet. I've got it locked in my office drawer."

"Do I have to call my father? Can't you just give it to me?"

"No. He's the one who should decide on the disposition of the effects, money included."

"He'll just say no, and I need the money for the car payment. He'll probably take the car, too, won't he?"

"Is the car in your brother's name?"

She nodded and began to cry. "It just isn't fair! We both worked hard to buy that car, to make the down payment and all, and now my father'll get it!"

"Maybe your brother left a will?"

"Why would he have a will? He was only twenty-one years old. He didn't expect to die from a broken finger! I still don't see how anybody can die from a broken finger."

45

"Let me explain," Hoke said. He finished the last bite of his sandwich and wiped his mouth with his napkin. "Dr. Evans is the best pathologist in America, and he's the best doctor and dentist, too. He said it wasn't the finger, but the shock that set in because of the broken finger. And if he says that, it's gospel. Let me tell you about Dr. Evans. 'Bout a year ago, I had some abscessed teeth, and the only way I could chew was to hold my head over to one side and chew like a dog on the side that didn't hurt. I was having lunch with Dr. Evans, and after lunch, he took me back to the morgue, shot me up with Novocaine, and pulled all my teeth. Every one of them. Then he made an impression and had these teeth made for me by the same technician who makes all of the Miami Dolphins' false teeth."

Hoke took out his dentures, put them on a napkin, and handed them to Susan.

"I didn't even know you had false teeth," Susan said. "Did you, Junior?"

"No, I didn't," Freddy said. "Let me take a look at those."

Susan passed the teeth to Freddy, and he examined them closely before giving them back to Hoke. "Nice," he said.

"I call 'em my Dolphin choppers," Hoke said. He sprinkled some water from his glass on his dentures, then slipped the dentures back into his mouth and adjusted them. "That's the kind of doctor Dr. Evans is—and he didn't charge me a dime. He just did it for the experience, he said. I went home after he pulled my teeth, drank a half of a fifth of bourbon, and didn't feel a thing.

"But to get back to the will, if your brother was a sworn-in Krishna, they might've had him make out a will for them. As I understand it, when you join the group, you're supposed to sign over everything you own to them. I'd better check that out."

"In that case, the Krishnas'll get the two hundred dollars and the car. Either way, I'll be shit out of luck, won't I?"

"Perhaps. His partner's notified them at the ashram by

46

now, so if he does have a will on file, they'll probably come down to the station tomorrow to see me. They may not know about the car, but his partner will know he collected some money out at the airport today. Just in case, I won't mention the car to them. As a Krishna, I know he isn't supposed to own a private vehicle. Does your father know about the car?"

"I don't know. But I don't think so."

"Don't worry about it, then. Just keep quiet, and make the payments. After a few months, or when it's paid for, you can get a lawyer to have it changed over to your name."

Hoke took out his wallet, shuffled through his card case, and handed Susan a business card. "When you need a lawyer, try this guy, Izzy Steinmetz. He costs a little more, just like the breath mints, but he's worth it." Hoke smiled at Freddy. "He's a good criminal lawyer, too, in case you ever get into trouble."

"Hang onto the card," Freddy said to Susan. "Maybe Mr. Steinmetz can help us when we get our Burger King franchise."

The waiter brought the check. Hoke took it, and left a $3 tip on the table. They walked over to the cashier by the double-doors. Hoke put the check and his credit card on the counter. The manager smiled, tore the check in half, and pushed the card back.

"Your credit's no good here, Sergeant Moseley. Why don't we see you in here more often? It's been quite a while now."

"I'm working days now, and living over at the Beach. I'll try to get by more often. Thanks, Aquilar."

"That was nice of him," Freddy said, after they were outside, "to tear up the check that way."

"But you noticed," Hoke said, "that I offered to pay. Aquilar's a nice guy. We go back a long way, and I did a favor for him once."

"What kind of a favor?"

"I called him on the phone. Where do you want me to drop you, Susan?"

"Second and Biscayne'll be fine."

Hoke dropped them off at the corner of Second and Biscayne. He started to make an illegal U-turn to get back to the MacArthur Causeway and then changed his mind. He didn't want to go home; he never wanted to go home. He continued down the boulevard and headed for the Dupont Plaza Hotel.

The pair had puzzled him. He had tried to jar them into some kind of reaction by showing them his Dolphin choppers, but they hadn't even risen above the level of mild curiosity. Cold fish. The jock was obviously an ex-con. There was no way that Mendez could be his real name. With that bronze tan, he looked like an Afrika Corps Nazi, and it was definitely a tan, not dark skin. Besides, the world was too fresh and new to him, as though he had been out of circulation for some time. The way he had crooked that Charles Atlas arm around the tiny cup of flan—who did he think would try to take it away from him, anyway? It wasn't enough that Carter had destroyed the city by sending in all the refugees, Reagan was importing ex-cons from California. Even if immigration was stopped altogether, it would be another twenty years before Miami got back to normal again.

And the girl. She had looked at her dead brother as if he were a piece of meat. True, she had cried at the morgue, but she had cried much harder about the possible loss of her car and the $200. How could a girl as simple-minded as Susan Waggoner get into college?

Hoke drove into the Dupont Plaza garage and parked on the ramp by the wall. As he locked the car, a Cuban attendant came running over. He had a parking stub in one hand, and a one-ounce hit of café Cubano in the other.

"I'll take those keys," he said, holding out the parking stub.

Hoke showed him his shield and ignored the stub.

"Police business. I'll leave the car right where it is. When more cars come in, drive around it."

Hoke went into the bar lounge, filled a paper plate with chicken wings, hot meatballs, and green olives, then went to the bar. He ordered a beer reluctantly because a beer in the Dupont Plaza bar cost as much as a six-pack in the supermarket, but the free hors d'oeuvres just about made up for it. Hoke liked the Dupont Plaza, the quiet Mickey Mouse music that came over the speakers, and the tables beside the windows where he could watch the traffic on the Miami River. There was an older, dressed-up crowd here, and although his blue poplin leisure suit was out of place, he had once picked up a forty-year-old widow from Cincinnati, and she had taken him up to her room.

Hoke showed the bartender his shield and asked for the telephone. The bartender reached under the bar and placed a white telephone in front of Hoke. As a matter of principle, Hoke never gave Ma Bell a quarter to use a pay telephone. He dialed Red Farris's number from memory.

"Red," Hoke said, when Farris answered, "let's go out and do something."

"Hoke! I'm glad you called. I tried to get you twice today, once at the station, and once at your hotel. The hotel didn't even answer."

"You've got to let it ring. Sometimes the clerk's away from the desk."

"I let it ring ten times."

"Try twenty next time. I was out at the airport most of the afternoon, on a homicide."

"How come they called you instead of Metro?"

"I'll tell you when I see you. It's an interesting case."

"That's why I tried to call you, Hoke, to tell you my good news. Are you ready? I resigned today."

"Resigned from the department? You're shitting me."

"Not this time, Hoke. I told you before I've been writing letters around the state. Well, the chief of police in Sebring offered me a job as desk sergeant, and I took it."

49

"That means going back into uniform, doesn't it?"

"So what? I'll be out of Miami. When I typed up my resignation, I never felt better."

"What kind of salary goes with it?"

"Not much."

"How much? Sebring can't pay Miami's union scale."

"I know. It's only fourteen thousand, Hoke. I'm making thirty-one in Robbery, but the chief said there'd probably be another two thousand a year when the new Sebring budget comes out."

"Christ, Red, that's less than half of what you're making now."

"I know, and I don't give a shit. It doesn't cost as much to live in Sebring, and the chances are that I'll live a hell of a lot longer up there."

"There's nothing going on in Sebring. They have the race once a year, and that's it."

"I know. That's why I took the job. Last week, a kid in Overtown threw a brick through my window."

"You shouldn't drive your car in Overtown. You know that."

"It was a squad car, Hoke. I was down there with Nelson to pick up a fence. We never found him, either. But that brick was it. I'd been wavering, because of the money and all, but the next morning I called the chief in Sebring. He's a nice guy, too, Hoke. You'd like him. He's a retired detective from Newark. That's in New Jersey."

"I know where Newark is, for God's sake."

"Don't get pissed off, Hoke."

"I'm not pissed off, I'm just surprised, that's all. I know damned well you aren't going to like living in a little town like that. Why don't we meet some place and talk about it?"

"I can't, Hoke. I've got a lot of things to do and then I've got to meet Louise later when she gets off work."

"When are you leaving, Red? I'll see you before you go, won't I?"

"Oh, sure. I'll be in town for another week at least. If I

50

can't sell my condo, I'll have to rent it out. But we'll get together. We'll tie one on to celebrate."

"Right. I'm here at the Dupont bar, if you can get away for a while before you pick up Louise."

"I can't, Hoke. Not tonight."

"Call me, then."

"I'll call you."

"I'm real happy for you, Red, if you think that's what you want."

"Thanks, Hoke. It's what I want."

"Call me."

"I will."

Hoke racked the phone, and the bartender put it beneath the bar again. "Another beer, sir?"

"Yeah. And a double shot of Early Times. I don't want any more of the stuff on this plate either. Can you dump it for me?"

Hoke took his shot of whiskey and fresh bottle of beer over to a table by the window. He really hated to see Red Farris leave the department. He was one of the few bachelor friends Hoke had left. Red was almost always available to go out for a few drinks, or a little bottle pool, or to bowl a few lines. And Red Farris had saved his life, too. They had gone to pick up a wife-beater who was out on bail. The man's wife had died, and that upgraded the charge from assault to second degree murder. It was a simple pickup; the man didn't put up any fight or argument. He had been too shocked by the news of his wife's death. And then, just as Hoke had started to put the handcuffs on him, the man's twelve-year-old son had come out of the bedroom and shot Hoke in the chest with a .22 rifle. Farris got the rifle out of the kid's hands before he could get off another shot, and Hoke spent six weeks in the hospital with a nicked left lung. It still hurt if he took a very deep breath. But if Red Farris hadn't twisted that rifle out of the kid's hands— Well, the kid was in a foster home somewhere, the kid's father was up in Raiford, and the boy's mother was dead. In Miami, a family could break up in a hurry.

It used to be a lot different when Hoke was still married. Four or five couples would get together for a barbecue and some beer. Then, after they ate, the women would all sit in the living room and talk about how difficult their deliveries had been, and the men would sit in the kitchen and play poker. The big kids would watch TV, and the smaller kids would be put to sleep in the bedroom. That had been real Florida living, but now all the white families were moving away. There were six different detectives Hoke had known who had left Miami in the last year alone. And now Farris— that was seven. Of course, Henderson could get out for a night once in a while, but Bill Henderson was married, and he always worried about staying out too late.

Hoke looked out at the river, never the same river. He wanted another double shot of Early Times, but not at these prices. Hoke left the bar and got his car from the parking ramp. As he checked the window locks, the smell of the vomit on the back seat was almost overpowering. When he got to the Eldorado Hotel, he'd get one of the Marielitos who lived there to clean it out.

7

THE ONE-WAY STREET was narrow after they left the well-lighted area of the Columbus Hotel on Biscayne. The sidewalk was cracked and broken from recent roadwork, and there were few pedestrians.

"Where's the parking garage?" Freddy took Susan's thin arm as they skirted a Bob's Barricade horse and a flaming kerosene pot.

"Up about four blocks. I didn't want the detective to see my car. I'm sorry now I even mentioned it to him. If he lets it slip out to daddy that I've got it, he'll take it."

"That prick detective's pretty sharp. Unless he does it on purpose, he won't let anything slip out. He sure picked up on me in a hurry. I think I had him fooled on the dessert business, because I really was in a foster home in Santa Barbara. But he knows that a man can't hold down a regular job and still work out six hours a day building up muscles like mine."

"Why'd you tell him your name was Ramon Mendez? You don't look nothing like these Cubans." She pointed to four ragged Marielitos across the street. They were unwrapping a large bundle of clothes between two parked cars.

"I told him Mendez because I checked into the hotel

53

under the name of Gotlieb with a stolen credit card. Wait. Let's go over there and see what they've got in that bindle."

"Let's don't! You don't want to have nothing to do with these people, Junior. It's just something they stole, anyway." She tugged at his arm.

"Okay. But it's always interesting to look into a bindle. You never know what you'll find."

"You mess with these Cubans and they'll pull a knife on you." At the next corner, they waited for the light to change. "If your name isn't Gotlieb, and it isn't Mendez, what is it?"

"Junior, like I told you. My last name's Frenger. I'm really German, I suppose, but I don't remember my parents. I was in four different foster homes, but no one ever told me anything about my parents. They said I was an orphan, but they could've been lying about that. They lied about everything else, so it's possible my parents are still alive somewhere. I've always thought my father must've been an important man, though, or he wouldn't't've named me Junior. At least that proves I'm not a bastard. You don't name a kid after yourself if you aren't married. What d'you think?"

"I'm too upset to think right now. On top of everything else, I think Mr. Turner's going to make us write a haiku, and I don't think I can do it."

"It seems simple enough to me. There're only seventeen syllables. Five, seven, and five. I'll write some for you, and you can keep 'em in your purse. Then, if he gives you a makeup paper in his office, you can copy them in your own handwriting."

"Suppose I have to explain what they mean?"

"I'll tell you what they mean after I write them."

"Would you?"

"Sure. We're engaged, aren't we?"

"Did you really mean that? When you told Mr. Turner we were engaged?"

"Why not? I've never even gone steady before."

They reached the six-story parking garage. Susan showed her parking pass to the attendant behind the bulletproof window. He took her keys from the board, raised the grate an inch, and slid them across the Formica countertop.

"I pay eighty dollars a month to park here. And that's the student rate. Some of these downtown lots charge three dollars an hour, and they make so much money they won't give you a monthly rate." They took the elevator to the fifth floor. "But they're nasty about it here. If I don't get here early enough in the morning to get a space, the garage fills up and they put out a full sign. So even though I've paid in advance, I still can't park. It isn't fair."

"You use that word a lot."

"What word?"

"*Fair.* Now that you're twenty years old—"

"Only by one month—"

"—you'd better forget about things like *fair* and *unfair.* Even when people talk about the weather, *fair* doesn't mean anything."

"But there's such a thing as—"

"No, there isn't. Jesus, is this your car?"

Susan unlocked the driver's door to a white 1982 TransAm. There was a flaming red bird decal on the hood and flowing red flames painted on all four of the fenders.

"It's mine now, if they don't take it away from me. It was the first thing we bought when we had enough saved for the down payment. Marty was crazy about it. But he only got to drive it two or three times. What he wanted was a car that would impress his friends when we went back to Okeechobee. That's why I'm pretty sure he never told daddy about the car. He wanted to surprise everybody. There are real leather seats, you know. Black glove leather. D'you want to drive, Junior?"

"No. I can drive, but I'm not a very good driver. And even though I've got three California licenses on me, I don't fit the descriptions. Besides, you'd have to tell me where to turn and all."

Freddy got into the passenger's soft bucket seat. He felt as though he were sitting in a deep pit, even though the visibility was excellent through the tinted front window. The side and back windows had been layered with chocolate film; they were almost black.

Susan started the engine. "I'll turn the air conditioning down in just a second. It'll really freeze your ass off if you leave it on high very long."

"Do you need gas? I've got Ramon Mendez's Seventy-six card."

"This thing always needs gas. It only gets about nine miles to a gallon. Something's wrong with the carburetor, I think."

"Well, don't worry about gas. I can get all of the gas credit cards we'll need."

Susan roared down the spiraling driveway and into the street. She drove through the streets aggressively, taking the Eighth Street ramp to the overhead freeway to South Dixie. But once on South Dixie, in three lanes, the traffic was heavy, and it was stop-and-go driving until they reached South Miami and Sunset Drive. The heavy traffic thinned out slightly when she turned west on Sunset.

"People can't see in at all, can they?" Freddy said.

"Not very well. To see inside you have to put your face right up against the glass."

"I haven't seen much of the city, either."

"You can't see much at night. I'll take you around to-morrow, anywhere you want to go."

They had the car filled at a Shell station. Freddy paid for the gas with Gotlieb's credit card. As the attendant wrote down the license number on the sales slip, Freddy shook his head. "I forgot they did that. Tomorrow we're going to either get some new license plates or a new car. We should've stopped along the way so I could've picked up some new license plates. I could've changed them before we got the gas."

Susan opened the door, jumped out, and dashed after the attendant. She got the credit slip back, and paid the man cash for the fuel. She got back into the driver's seat and tore up the credit slip.

"I'll probably lose the car, but we might as well keep it as long as we can."

"That was quick thinking, Susie. I'm so used to using credit cards, I never thought about paying cash."

"I always pay cash. Still, I try not to carry more'n fifty dollars on me at a time."

"Tomorrow I'll get us some out-of-state plates we can switch. And tomorrow night I'd better get some Miami credit cards. I'll get some for you, too, some ladies' cards, so you can buy things when I'm not around."

THERE WERE THIRTY four-story condominium apartment buildings in the complex that made up Kendall Pines Terrace, but only six of the buildings had been completed and occupied. The other buildings were unpainted, windowless, concrete shells. Construction had been suspended for more than a year. Almost all of the apartments in the occupied buildings were empty. For the most part, their owners had purchased them at preconstruction prices during the real estate boom in 1979. But now, in fall 1982, construction prices had risen, and very few people could qualify for loans at 17 percent interest.

"There's been some vandalism out here," Susan said, when she parked in her numbered space in the vast and almost empty parking lot. "So they built a cyclone fence and hired a Cuban to drive around at night in a Jeep. That's stopped it. But sometimes, late at night, it's a little scary out here."

There was a tropical courtyard in the hollow square of Building Six-East. Broad-leaved plants had been packed in thickly around the five-globed light in the center of the patio, and cedar bark had been scattered generously around the plants. There was a pleasant tingle of cedar and night-blooming jasmine in the air.

Susan had a corner two-bedroom, two-bath apartment with a screened porch facing the Everglades. There was eggshell wall-to-wall carpet throughout the apartment, except for the kitchen, which had a linoleum floor in a white brick pattern. Both bathrooms had been tiled in blue and pink. The furniture in the living room was rattan, with blue-and-green striped cushions. There was a large brass bed in the master bedroom. In the smaller bedroom, Susan's, there was a Bahama bed and a rattan desk. There were antique white Levolors in all of the windows, but no curtains or draperies.

While Freddy looked around the apartment, Susan got two San Miguel beers out of the refrigerator. She took Freddy out to the screened porch and pointed toward the dark Everglades.

"In the daytime you can see them, but not now. For the next four miles or so those are all tomato and cucumber fields. Then you get to Krome Avenue, and beyond that it's the East Everglades—nothing but water and alligators. It gets too drowned with water to build on the other side of Krome, and Kendall Pines Terrace is the last complex in Kendall. Eventually, the rest of those fields will all be condos, because Kendall is the chicest neighborhood in Miami. But they won't be able to build anymore in the 'Glades unless they drain them."

"This apartment looks expensive."

"It is, for the girl that owns it. She put every cent she had into it, and then found out she couldn't afford to live here. She's just a legal secretary, so she had to rent it out, furniture and all. We only pay her four hundred a month rent, but she was glad to get it. She tried to sell or rent it for four months before we came along. Even with our four hundred, she still has to come up with another four-fifty every month."

"Where does she live now?"

"She had to move back with her parents in Hallandale, and she's twenty-five years old. I know how bad she feels. I'd never move back in with daddy. I'd rather die first."

"This is good beer."

"San Miguel dark. It's the best, and it comes all the way from the Philippine Islands. The man at Crown gets it for me. Of course, in addition to the four hundred a month, the electric bill comes to another two hundred."

"No shit?"

Susan nodded. "On account of the air conditioning. And it'll be going up again soon. The anchorette on Channel Ten said so last night. Without the money from Marty coming in, I don't think I can handle it. I'm worried."

"Don't be. We're engaged, so I'll take care of it."

Freddy put his fingers on the screen. The dead man in the morgue was sure as hell the same guy at the airport. He hadn't meant to kill him; all he had wanted to do was break the guy's finger. Just because of the jacket, and now he didn't even have the leather jacket with him. What he did have was the simple-minded younger sister. He could feel the damp jets of air coming through the screen. There were only six cars parked in the ten-acre parking lot. The white TransAm, in its numbered slot, seemed to glow in the sixth row. Every other parking light in the lot had been turned off, to save energy, perhaps, and the other lights had been dimmed. The moon wasn't up yet, and beyond the cyclone fence was blackness. Looking out and down into the dark land mass, Freddy felt as if he were on the edge of an abyss. Perspiration from his armpits trickled down his sides.

"Let's go back inside," Freddy said. "Doesn't it even cool off at night?"

"A little. Around four in the morning it'll drop down to seventy-seven or so, but then the humidity'll go up."

Freddy took off his shoes and his shirt. Susan sat on the couch in the living room. "D'you want to watch some TV, Junior?"

"Not now. I've got to make a phone call. Where's the telephone book?"

"There's two books over there, under the breakfast table. The phone's on the—"

"I can see the phone."

Freddy looked up the number of the International Hotel. He called the desk, checked out, and told the clerk to charge everything, including his barber bill, to his Gotlieb credit card. "Yes," he finished, "I did have a pleasant stay."

Freddy joined Susan on the couch and told her to bring him a pair of scissors. He cut up the Gotlieb credit and identification cards, and put the cut pieces into the ashtray.

"Now," he said, "Mr. Gotlieb's no longer in Miami."

Freddy patted the lounge, and Susan sat beside him. "I liked the way you handled yourself at the morgue, Susan. What were you thinking about, anyway, when you saw your dead brother?"

"I was thinking about the times when he used to bend my fingers back when he wanted me to do something. It really hurt, and after a while he didn't have to bend them back. All he had to do was threaten to do it, and I'd do whatever he wanted. He was religious, I guess, but he was awfully mean. He said he wanted to go to heaven, and now he's got what he wanted." She was lost in thought for a moment, then she looked up.

"What I want to do, first thing tomorrow, is go down to the bank and take out the CD. Then I can start another one some place else. We've got a ten-thousand-dollar CD saved, plus another four thousand in our joint NOW account. And I sure don't want daddy or the Krishnas to get it."

"Good. We'll do that first thing. Now that we're engaged, we're going to start our platonic marriage. D'you know what that is?"

Susan nodded. "Beth had one, on 'The Days of Our Lives,' when she moved in with the lawyer. And I want one too. I've been really lonely out here at night. I didn't like Marty, but even so, I missed him when he moved out to the camp."

"Why didn't you like him? He was your brother."

"Remember, before, when I told you I never went steady? Marty's why, that's why. He's the one that got me pregnant, and I think daddy suspicioned it, too. And then when we came down to Miami and I got the abortion, Marty couldn't find any work. He met Pablo when he was looking for work at the hotel. So then he made me go to work for Pablo. I don't like working at the hotel, Junior, I really don't. That old man from Dayton, Ohio, today was disgusting."

"You've turned your last trick for Pablo. You're living with me now."

"You really don't know Pablo. He smiles and bows and all that, but he's mean. And he knows where I—where we live, Junior."

"Don't worry about Pablo. I'll take care of him. Do you remember that Bob Dylan song about the lady laying across a brass bed?"

"I don't remember. Maybe I did. They don't play much Dylan on the radio anymore."

"Well, here's what you do. Go into the bedroom, take off your clothes, put two pillows under your stomach, and lay face down on the big brass bed. I'm gonna have another beer, and then I'll be right in."

"You're gonna do it to me the back way whether I want to or not, aren't you?"

"Yeah."

"In that case, I'd better get another San Miguel for you, and some Crisco for me."

LATER, BARS OF moonlight came through the slanted vertical Levolors and made yellow bars across Freddy's hairless chest. Susan, in a shorty nightgown, snuggled close to him and used his extended right arm as a pillow. Freddy chuckled deep in his throat and then snorted.

"Remember that haiku the teacher wrote?"

"Not exactly," Susan said.

"*The Miami sun/Rising in the Everglades/Burger in a bun*. That's what I was laughing at. Now I know what it means."

8

THERE WAS A middle-aged man sitting in the glass-walled office with Sergeant Bill Henderson when Hoke arrived in the squad room. Hoke checked his mailbox and then signaled his presence to Henderson with a wave of his arm. Henderson beckoned for him to come over. Henderson got to his feet and smiled as Hoke crossed the crowded squad room. Most of Henderson's front teeth were reinforced with silver inlays, and his smile was a sinister grimace. Hoke and Bill had been working together for almost four years, and Hoke knew that when Henderson smiled, something horrible about human nature had been reconfirmed for his partner.

Hoke cracked open the door. "I'm going down for coffee, Bill. I'll be right back."

"I already got you coffee." Henderson pointed to the capped Styrofoam cup on Hoke's side of the double desk. "I want you to meet Mr. Waggoner. We've been having an interesting little chat here, and I know you'll want to hear what he's got to say."

Hoke shook hands and sat in his chair. "Sergeant Moseley. I'm Sergeant Henderson's partner."

"Clyde Waggoner. I'm Martin's father." The man from

Okeechobee was wearing a white rayon tie with a blue chambray work shirt, and khaki trousers. There was a thin nylon Sears windbreaker folded over his left arm. He had short brown hair with shaved temples, the kind of haircut they call white sidewalls in the armed forces. His skin was sallow, but it was blotchy in places from long exposure to the Florida sun, and there were scars on his nose and cheeks from debrided skin cancers.

"I suppose you came for your son's effects," Hoke said, unlocking his desk drawer. "Sorry I'm a little late this morning, but I had to drop off some dry cleaning."

Mr. Waggoner looked down at his scuffed engineer boots, made a goatlike sound in his throat, and began to cry. The sound was softly muffled, but the tears that came down his blotchy cheeks were genuine. Hoke directed a puzzled look at Henderson, and his partner broadened his brutal smile.

"Just tell Sergeant Moseley the same story you told me, Mr. Waggoner. I could summarize it, but I might leave something out."

Mr. Waggoner blew his nose on a blue bandanna and stuffed the handkerchief into his left hip pocket. He wiped his cheeks with his fingers.

"I can't prove nothing, sergeant, as I told Sergeant Henderson here. All I can tell you is what I think happened. I hope I'm wrong, I surely do hope so. My business is bad enough already, and a scandal like this could make it worse. Okeechobee's a small town, and our moral standards are a lot different up there than they are down here in Miami. You know what they call Miami up in Okeechobee?"

"No, but I don't suppose it's complimentary."

"It ain't. They call it Sin City, Sergeant Moseley."

"Are you, perhaps, a man of the cloth?"

"No, sir. Software. I got me a software store in Okeechobee. I sell video games, computers, and rent out TV sets and movies."

"My father owns a hardware store in Riviera Beach," Hoke said.

"He's smarter than me, then. What I had in mind when I opened the store was a computer business for the commercial fishing on the lake. The government sets quotas, you see, and I figured if the fish houses had computers they could always prove exactly how much fish they caught and all that. Plus they'd know when they was falling behind, and so on. Then last year, when the lake went down to nine feet, the government stopped commercial fishing almost altogether. No nets allowed, you see, so all the fish houses're just about out of business now. Besides, nobody's buying computers up there because there ain't no programs written up for lake fishing anyway."

"So you're just about out of business, right?"

"Oh, no—I'm doing all right. But I borrowed money to expand, and the interest is hurting me. My movie rental club alone pays my rent each month, but I'm in pretty heavy to the bank, you see. But I ain't here to talk business. What I was telling Sergeant Henderson here is that I suspect foul play."

"What kind of foul play?"

"That was no accident that killed Martin. That was murder."

"If so, it's the first of a kind."

"Let him finish," Henderson said. "There's more."

"That's the best kind," Mr. Waggoner continued, "the kind that looks like an accident but really ain't. I've seen it on 'The Rockford Files' more'n once, and if it wasn't for Jim Rockford, a lot of people'd get away with it, too."

"What makes you think your son's death wasn't an accident?"

"I'd really rather not talk about it because it's so painful to me, as a father, you see. But I'm also a good citizen, and justice, no matter how harsh, must be done. Even to kith and kin . . ." He started to cry again, softer this time, and reached for his handkerchief.

Hoke took the plastic lid off his coffee and sipped it. It was cold. "When did you get this coffee?"

"I got in a little early today," Henderson said. "But I didn't know you'd be a half-hour late."

Hoke replaced the plastic lid and dropped the cup of coffee into the wastebasket. He lit a cigarette, took a long drag, and butted the cigarette in the ashtray as he allowed the smoke to trickle out through his nose.

"So you think, Mr. Waggoner," Hoke said, "that this unidentified assailant who broke your son's middle finger killed him on purpose? Is that right?"

"That's about the size of it." Mr. Waggoner blew his nose, examined his handkerchief, and then put it back into his pocket. "I think the man, whosoever he was, was hired to do it. That's what I think."

"The chances of killing a man that way are pretty remote, Mr. Waggoner. I doubt if more than one man in a thousand—I don't know the actual statistics—would die from a trauma to his finger. It would be pretty stupid to hire someone to kill anybody in that manner."

"You might be right about that. But if a man was hired to injure somebody on purpose, and then that person died because of the injury, wouldn't that be a murder for hire?"

"A case could be made for that, I suppose. Except for a thousand unidentified passengers a day who don't like Hare Krishnas, who hated your son enough to hire someone to break his middle finger?"

"That's what's so painful to me." Mr. Waggoner sighed. "I think my daughter hired him."

Hoke took the morgue identification form out of his notebook, unfolded it, and placed it on the desk. "Susan, the daughter who identified the body? Or do you have another daughter in mind?"

"No. Susan's the only daughter I got. And Martin was my only son. None of us got along too good, I'll admit that, and I sent her packing when she got pregnant. But Martin, even though he's the one that done it to her, was my only son, and she shouldn't've had him killed. Susan's just like her mother, who was no good either, so I know she talked

Martin into doing it to her in the first place." Mr. Waggoner lowered his voice and his head. "Men are weak. I know that because I'm weak when it comes to women myself. We all are, even you two gentlemen, if you don't mind my saying so. A woman can make you do anything she wants you to do with that there little hair-pie they've got between their legs. I know it, and you know it, too."

"Let me get this straight," Hoke said. "Your own son impregnated his sister, your daughter, Susan, and then Susan hired someone to kill him for revenge. Is that right?"

"That's right. Yes, sir."

"And where's the baby?"

"Susan had her an abortion here in Miami. I gave her eight hundred dollars when I sent her down here to get it. You can check that out easy enough, and Martin went with her, telling me he'd come back. He never did, though."

"Are you positive Martin was the father?"

"No doubt about that. They was alone in the house all the time, and Martin, he never let her go out with no one else. I didn't see what was going on at first. I just thought he was protecting her from those other boys up there, the way a big brother'll look after his little sister. But after they left, I looked around the house some, and I found things. Martin, pretending to be so religious and all—butter beans wouldn't melt in his mouth—had two French ticklers hid in his old high school Blue Horse notebook way back in the closet. And they was other things, too . . ." He looked at the toes of his boots and whispered. "Noises in the night . . . you know the kind. Down deep, I guess I must've known what they was up to all along, but I didn't want to believe it, so I pretended it was something else.

"I don't fear God or no man. What I fear is that little hair-pie, that's what I fear. And knowing what I know, and knowing what kind of girl Susie is, a sneaky little girl, I just know she got her revenge on Martin. But as I said, I can't prove nothing. I had to tell you what I think. The rest is up to you. I just hope you prove I'm wrong."

"If I type up a statement about your suspicions," Henderson said, "will you sign it?"

"Well, no. I told you, and that should be enough. I'll sign for Martin's effects, though. I know I've got to do that."

"I'm sorry," Hoke said, "but in view of what you've told us, we're going to hang on to them for a while. At least until we complete the investigation."

"Including the money? Sergeant Henderson said Martin had more'n two hundred dollars in his wallet."

"That's right. The money, too. He might've left a will, and in that case the money'll go into probate."

"I understand. I guess that's the price a man pays for doing his duty. How do I get the body?"

"It depends upon when they finish the post-mortem. But you can notify any funeral director to take care of it for you. If you want a cremation, the Neptune Society will do it for you and scatter his ashes at sea."

"Can't I get the ashes myself? I'd like to scatter 'em on the lake. Martin always loved the lake as a boy, so that's where he'd like to be scattered."

"You can do whatever you like. You don't, by law, have to have the body embalmed, so don't let anybody talk you into that, Mr. Waggoner. Thank you for coming in." Hoke stood up, and so did Mr. Waggoner.

"You'll let me know, then, how the investigation comes out?"

"No. All our inquiries will be confidential. If the investigation's negative, it would be foolish to let anyone know we made one in the first place. So you don't have to worry about any publicity."

"I may not look it," Mr. Waggoner said, "but I'm ashamed. I'm deeply ashamed of what I had to tell you. Thank you both for being so patient."

"I'll take you to the elevator," Henderson said. "It's easy to get turned around in this building."

* * *

HENDERSON TOOK A glazed doughnut out of his desk drawer, broke it in half, and offered the smaller half to Hoke. Hoke shook his head, and Henderson began to eat the doughnut.

"How'd you like Mr. Waggoner's little story, Hoke?"

"I found the bit about the hair-pie instructive."

"Me, too. Although I knew already that I was weak in that regard. You ever been in Okeechobee?"

"Years ago. But not since I left Riviera Beach. My dad and I went fishing for catfish on the lake a few times, but we only went into the town a couple of times. There's nothing much there, or there wasn't ten years ago. It's just an elbow bend on the highway north. I wouldn't think the town could support a software store, even if Waggoner rents out film for TV. But for all I know, Okeechobee's probably tripled in size by now, just like every other town in Florida the last few years. If a man likes to fish, it wouldn't be a bad place to retire."

"Apparently, there's a shortage of women. Otherwise, a brother wouldn't have to screw his own sister."

"You know I spent some time with the girl, Susan, last night, and there might be some truth to what Waggoner told us."

"Bullshit. If you hire somebody in Miami to do a beating for you, you get a professional job with bicycle chains. You don't pay anyone fifty bucks to break a lousy finger."

"But wouldn't a girl be chicken-hearted and not want her big brother hurt too badly?"

"Anything's possible. You want to check it out? We've got better things to do, you know."

"Susan's boyfriend was with her when I took her down to the morgue. He's an ex-con, I'm positive, and strong enough to break someone's *arm*. He gave me a phony name, Ramon Mendez, and for no good reason that I could see— unless he's on the run."

"Did you run a make on the name?"

"On Mendez? We've got hundreds of them. Remember when we tried to get a make on José Perez? Twenty-seven with records popped up. These Latins all have four last names and a half-dozen first names, including at least one saint on the list. And they use the ones they want at the time. But this boyfriend isn't a Latin in the first place. Remember the intelligence seminar we went to last year, the one the agent from Georgia gave? He was with the GBI."

"I remember that sonofabitch all right. He learned my name in the first class and called on me at every session."

"Well, Susan's boyfriend had blue eyes just like his—flat and staring. And he never looked away. I'd planned to lean on him a little, but after we talked for a while I knew I'd be wasting my time. Now, if Susan asked him to, this guy would break her brother's finger or neck without even thinking about it. He's done time, I'm sure, and he might even be a fugitive. He says he's from California, here to study management at Miami-Dade."

"That's possible. People come from all over the world to study at Miami-Dade."

"Not from California. In California, you can go to college free. So why would a man come three thousand miles to pay out-of-state fees at Miami-Dade?"

"You can go to college free in California?"

"That's right, right on through a bachelor's."

"Why don't you check him out, then, at Miami-Dade?"

"I will. But I'll have to find out what his right name is first." Hoke got up, and pushed his chair into the desk kneehole.

"Is that where you're going now?"

"No. I'm going down to the cafeteria for some coffee and a doughnut."

9

SUSAN MADE SCRAMBLED eggs with green peppers, buttered rye toast, and fried baloney slices for Freddy's breakfast. After he finished eating, he took his cup of coffee out to the screened porch. The brown, cultivated fields stretched out for several miles, and there were bands of dusty green that faded into a misty, darker green toward the horizon. The country was so incredibly flat he couldn't get over it. There wasn't a single mound or a dip or a gully for as far as he could see. And, from the fourth floor, the horizon had to be at least twenty or twenty-five miles away. Susie's apartment was on the western side of the building and shaded in the morning, but he knew that the sun would bake this side all afternoon.

Inside, with the air conditioning set on seventy-five, the apartment was nice and cool. Out on the porch, where the humid heat was at least eighty-five, the sudden change brought a shock to his skin. But he decided he liked the heat. Freddy didn't wear any underwear, and his linen slacks stuck to the backs of his legs as he sat in the plastic-webbed porch rocker. Susan, wearing white shorts and a light blue bikini halter, brought out the coffeepot and refilled his cup.

Her bare feet were long and narrow, and she looked about thirteen years old.

"Explain about the bank business again," Freddy said.

"It isn't a bank, it's a savings and loan, but it works just like a bank. I don't know the exact difference except that the S and L pays a higher interest rate. Marty and me got a CD for ten thousand in both our names, and a NOW checking account. The interest from the CD goes into our checking account automatically at the end of each month. There's more'n four thousand in it. So I'm going to draw it all out and start another CD and another NOW account in some other S and L. That way they won't be able to get none of it because it'll all be in my name."

"That's no good," Freddy said, shaking his head. "They can still sue you, those Krishnas with their lawyers, and then they'll tie up all the money until the judge decides who gets it. What you do, when you go down there, is take out all the money and bring it to me. I'll take care of it."

"That's too much money to keep around in cash. In Miami, somebody'll steal it from you."

"I'll rent a safe-deposit box, except for some walking around money. I don't want you to worry about it. What you don't have, they can't take away from you." He finished his coffee, handed her the cup. "Now that we've got our platonic marriage going, I'll take care of you. Don't you worry about interest or anything else. If you want something, anything—and I don't mean just because you *need* something, I mean *want* something—tell me, and I'll get it for you. Who's that guy down there?" Freddy pointed to a man wearing a dark blue suit, complete with vest, getting into a new Buick Skylark in the parking lot.

"I don't know his name. He lives down in two-fourteen, and he carried some groceries up here for me once. He's a prephase real estate salesman, he told me. That's why he has to wear a suit and tie all the time."

"What's a prephase salesman?"

"I don't know, but that's what he said he was. He seemed very nice and said he had a daughter about my age in junior high back in Ohio. I didn't tell him how old I was or proposition him. I don't think it's a good idea to fuck people where you have to live."

"You'd better get going to the S and L. So go ahead and get dressed."

"I am dressed. You don't have to get all dressed up out here in Kendall. All the women out here wear shorts and halters."

"Except you. I don't want my wife running around like some little kid. Put on a dress and shoes and stockings. Do something about your hair, too. It's all tangled."

"Aren't you going with me?"

"No. I'm going to study the street map of Miami. We'll go out when you come back."

FREDDY WATCHED SUSAN drive out of the parking lot. He put on his shirt, but not his shoes, and took the fire stairs down to the second floor. He twisted the knob of the front door to 214 as far as it would go, and then forced the door open with his shoulder. It sprung open easily.

He found two $100 bills in the bible on the bedside table and a loaded .38 caliber pistol in its leather holster in the drawer of the same table. There was a locked drawer in the metal home desk in the living room, but he found the key in the middle pencil drawer. He opened the locked drawer and found a cowhide case containing fifty silver dollars, each mounted in a round numbered slot. This was a collection, and much more valuable, he knew, than the $50 face value. When he rented the safe-deposit box, it might be a good idea to keep the collection to use as getaway bread. He took two pairs of black silk socks from the dresser and put his stolen items into a brown paper grocery sack he got from a stack under the kitchen sink. He added a package of six frozen pork chops from the freezer compartment to the sack, then returned to his own apartment.

The clothes in the salesman's closet, unhappily, had been at least two sizes too large for Freddy, but he was satisfied with his haul, especially with the pistol. He put the pork chops on the kitchen table so they would thaw for dinner. Then he shaved with a disposable lady's shaver Susan had unwrapped for him, and took a long tub bath.

Soaking in the tub, Freddy examined the Miami city map, section by section, from Perrine to North Bay Village. The greater Miami area was five times longer than it was wide, a long narrow urban strip hugging the coast and the bay, with no way to expand unless the buildings were built higher and higher. There was no way the city could expand any farther into the Everglades until they were drained, and the coastline was completely filled. If a man had to escape from the cops, he could only drive north or south. Only two roads crossed the Everglades to Naples, and both of these could be blocked. If a man drove south he would be caught, eventually, in Key West, and the cops could easily bottle up a man on the highways if he headed north, especially if he tried to take the Sunshine Parkway.

The only way to escape from anyone, in case he had to, would be to have three or four hidey-holes. One downtown, one in North Miami, and perhaps a place over in Miami Beach. There would be no other safe method to get away except by going to ground until whatever it was that he'd have done was more or less forgotten about. Then, when the search was over, he could drive or take a cab to the airport and get a ticket to anywhere he wanted to go.

Well, Freddy thought, I've already got me a nice little hidey-hole out here in Kendall.

Susan returned before noon with two bags of groceries and $4,280 in fifties and twenties. Freddy sat at the uncleared breakfast table and counted the money while Susan began to put away the groceries.

"It's ten thousand dollars short," he said.

"That's because I took out another CD at the S and L in

Miller Square. There's plenty of money right there to spend or to lock away in a safe-deposit box, without losing interest on the other ten thousand every month. There was already a penalty of almost four hundred dollars I had to pay for cashing in the CD early. I had to pay the penalty, but it's stupid not to have the interest coming in every month. I was getting one-thirty-two a month before, but the new S and L's only paying ninety-two." Susan picked up the package of frozen pork chops and frowned. "That's funny, I don't remember getting—"

Without rising, Freddy slapped Susan a sharp blow across the face. She fell down, dropping the pork chops, and the package slid across the linoleum floor. She began to cry and to rub her reddened cheek, which began to swell immediately.

"Part of being married," Freddy explained, "is learning to do exactly what your platonic husband tells you to do. I'm not some daddy you can defy, and I'm not a dumb brother you can manipulate. Do you know what 'manipulate' means?"

Susan nodded through her tears. "Uh-huh. I saw a program on it once, on 'Donahue.'"

"I'm not unreasonable. You're probably right about the interest rate and all. I don't know much about things like that. But the main thing here is that you didn't do what I told you to do. And you weren't really concerned about the interest rate, either. You kept the other ten thousand because you didn't trust me. Don't say anything. Not a word. I don't want to hear any lies. What I'm going to do, I'm going to let you keep the other ten thousand in the S and L. I don't need it right now, and you don't need it, and I realize you're insecure and need the money for your peace of mind. Now, put the pork chops back on the table and leave them there so they'll thaw out. I'll want them for dinner tonight, with whatever else you fix that'll go good with the pork chops."

"Will baked sweet potatoes be all right?"

"That's your department. Now, aren't you going to ask me where I got the pork chops?"

"I figure that's none of my business."

"That's right. Now you're learning."

Freddy looked through Susan's purse and took out the car keys. "I'm going down to the hotel to fix things up with Pablo for you. Then I'm going to get oriented around town. I should be back around six—that is, if I don't get lost. But I've checked out the map, and I don't think I will as long as I keep the avenues and the streets straight."

"I'm supposed to go to social science tonight. English on Monday and Wednesday, and social science on Tuesday and Thursday nights."

"No, I don't think so. I don't want you in school right now. Call up and tell your science teacher there's been a death in the family. Professor Turner already knows. I'll decide whether I want you to go back at all."

Freddy counted off a thousand dollars and pushed the rest of the money across the table. "Here." He folded the bills in half and put the roll into his right front pocket. "Take the rest of the money and stash it in a safe place somewhere in the apartment."

Freddy turned at the door. "One other thing. Call a locksmith and have him come out and put a deadbolt lock on the door. These push-button locks are engraved invitations for burglars."

"I already checked on deadlocks, and they cost more than sixty dollars. Is that all right? To pay that much, I mean?"

Freddy pointed to the stack of money on the table. "What would you rather lose? Sixty dollars, or all of that?" He pushed in the button on the doorknob, and closed the door gently behind him as he left.

Susan, slightly dazed, opened the refrigerator, stared into its depths for a moment, closed the door, took a roll of toilet paper out of the grocery sack, looked at it, dropped it back inside, started toward the bathroom, changed her mind, and then ran swiftly to the South Miami telephone book and turned to the Yellow Pages.

10

HOKE MOSELEY AND Bill Henderson sat close together on a pink silk loveseat in the living room of 11K, a townhouse in the Tahitian Village. Two-bedroom townhouses in the Tahitian Village started at $189,000, and the owners of this three-bedroom townhouse had also put out a good deal of money for the Latin Baroque furnishings. There were twisted, ornate bars on all of the downstairs windows. The interior color scheme was predominantly purple and rose. The wall-to-wall carpeting was richly purple, and the color was echoed without subtlety in the violet velvet draperies. The thick draperies hung in deep folds from two-headed iron spears in the living and dining rooms.

In the purple living room, two men, definitely Latins, with their hands and feet bound with copper wire, were face down on the floor. They had both been shot in the back of the head, and their faces were unrecognizable. A dark-haired young woman wearing a black-and-white maid's uniform, complete with a white frilly cap, had been shot in the hallway that led to the kitchen. Her hands and feet were also bound with copper wire. A small boy, two, or possibly three years old, had been shot in the head, but the child did not have his hands and feet bound. He was in the sunken bathtub in the rose-tiled bathroom on the second floor.

There was considerable activity in the townhouse. The forensic crew was busy. Two technicians were dusting for fingerprints, and another man was taking flash photographs from various angles. The ME, Dr. Merle Evans, was sitting at the glass-topped wrought-iron table in the dining room and writing notes on his clipboard.

The lady of the house, who had been out shopping at the Kendall Lakes Mall, said that she had returned to find her husband, her brother, the boy, and her maid dead. A Colombian with only rudimentary English, she had become hysterical. When he arrived, Doc Evans had given her a shot and sent her in an ambulance to the American Hospital emergency room.

After a quick initial look at the scene, Hoke Moseley and Bill Henderson had knocked on the nearby doors in the Tahitian Village, dividing up the townhouses, asking questions, and now they were comparing notes.

"No one I talked to," Henderson said, "heard or saw anything."

"I didn't do any better. These people here apparently kept to themselves, and I couldn't find anyone who knew or talked to them. They spoke Spanish and nothing else. Sometimes, in the morning, the maid took the little boy to the pool, but the adults never used the pool. And that's where the people of this complex get acquainted. A Colombian corporation, the manager told me, owns this townhouse, pays all the bills and maintenance, and people just come and go. When they come, they've got a letter in Spanish authorizing their stay, and he hands over the keys. When they leave, one of them returns the keys. He's never had any trouble with any of the tenants, he claims. They're always nice, quiet tenants, or so he says."

"Did he have their names?"

"No. The letter he showed me just said to admit the

bearers for an extended stay. I don't read Spanish, but he does, and that's what the letter said."

"He wouldn't lie about something like that," Henderson said, "but we can check it out, anyway. There had to be at least four shots, but no one heard even one. I can't get over that."

"Maybe it's a good thing they didn't hear the shots and come running out. Chances are, they'd be dead, too."

"Somebody had to hear something. They just don't want to get involved, that's all."

Doc Evans joined them. "They've been dead about two hours. That may not be exact, but from the body temperatures, I'm not far off."

Hoke nodded. "That coincides with what the woman said. She was gone for about two hours, and they were all alive when she left. I hope you can find some evidence of heroin when you open 'em up, doc. There's no dope in the apartment. Without some indication of dope, we can't say positively that the killings are drug-related. We can say that we think they are, but that isn't the same. If they're dope-related, nobody gives a shit, but if this was a murder-robbery, all these folks living out here'll get panicky."

"It's obviously a professional job," Doc said. "Too bad about the kid, though. At his age, he couldn't've identified anybody anyway."

"Colombian drug families are like that, doc," Henderson said. "They kill everyone in the family. They have to do it. If they hadn't killed the boy, someday, as a man, he'd kill them. When can I talk to the woman at the hospital?"

"Any time. She'll be a little dopey, but she can talk now. Why?"

"I've got a theory. I think she knew the killers. I also think they killed these people here, and then she drove them to the airport to catch a plane. Then she drove back here to report the bodies. As soon as she knew they were safely away, she called the department."

"Jesus, Bill," Hoke said, "you don't seriously believe

80

that a mother would help the killers of her own child get away, do you?"

"Well, how do we know it's her child? Life is cheap for those fuckers in Colombia. They might've brought the kid along with that plan in mind all along. Anyway, that's what I think, and I've got another reason besides. I'll take Martinez along to use as an interpreter."

"Why not? I'll wait here. I asked Kossowski from Narcotics to get a warrant so we can search her Caddy. She went shopping, she said, but I didn't see any packages in the car. If there's nothing in the trunk, your theory might be better than I think right now. Anyway," Hoke finished, "after we search the car, I'll call you at American."

"I'm going to lean on her." Henderson got to his feet. "Maybe their passports are in the trunk, too. There's not a scrap of ID in the house."

"The killers probably took the passports. But go ahead. You're bound to find out more than we know now."

KOSSOWSKI, TOGETHER WITH an assistant state attorney, arrived a few minutes later with a search warrant for the purple Cadillac. Kossowski and Hoke searched the car. The car was leased, not owned, and was very clean. There was nothing in the trunk except for a set of tools. There was a neatly folded map of Miami in the glove compartment and a well-chewed cigar in the ashtray. There were no pen or pencil markings on the map.

"This kind of search doesn't mean much, Hoke," Kossowski said. "When I get it downtown and take it apart, if there's a single grain of horse I'll find it."

"Take it, then. I think Henderson's on to something."

Hoke called the American Hospital and had Henderson paged. He was in the emergency room.

"Bill," Hoke said, "the car, on a perfunctory search here, was clean. I told Kossowski to take it downtown for a vacuum job. There were no packages in the trunk. It might be a good idea for you to twist the woman's arm."

"I've been trying, but all I get is *nunca*, like it was the only word she knows."

"Find out what her husband and her brother were doing in Miami."

"They were on vacation, she said."

"That isn't good enough."

"Martinez told me we should threaten to take her out to Krome to the alien detention camp and turn her over to the INS. She has no papers, and as an illegal alien, a few days living with those Haitian women out there might get her to talking."

"Don't just threaten her. If she won't say anything, take her out there and let the INS have her. Tell them she might harm herself, and they can slap her in solitary for a couple of days."

"As soon as we can get her out of emergency and into a private room, I'll be able to get tougher. There's no problem getting her a room—she's got nine hundred dollars in her purse. The hospital'll be glad to give her a private room until her money runs out."

"Whatever you decide, Bill, it's okay by me. Evans is taking the bodies now, and the forensic crew's almost finished. I'll wait around and seal up the townhouse, and check with the morgue later. Then I'll call you."

TWO HOURS LATER, Hoke stopped at a restaurant in Kendall Lakes. He had eaten his usual diet breakfast (one poached egg, one slice of dry toast, and coffee) but nothing since. It was almost four-thirty when he looked over the menu of Roseate Spoon Bill of Fare, a popular short-order restaurant in the rambling shopping center. When it came to eating, Hoke had a major problem. He had lost weight the year before, dropping from 205 to 185 pounds, and he wanted to keep it off, but at the same time he was always hungry. He could stick to his diet for two days at most, and then he went overboard on meat and mashed potatoes. With his new teeth, he could chew almost anything.

After a prolonged study of the wide-ranging menu, he decided to compromise. He ordered a Spanish omelet with cottage cheese instead of french fries, a dish of applesauce, and told the waitress to hold the toast.

While he waited, Hoke leafed through his notebook and tried to organize his thoughts. He crossed out the name of Ronald I. France. He could do nothing to help him; the grand jury had decided to prosecute this old man for shooting and killing a twelve-year-old boy who had ripped up his flower bed. The old man was seventy-two years old, and he had cried when Hoke had taken him in for booking. According to the neighbors, he had been a nice old man, but killing a kid for ripping up a flower bed had been too drastic. It didn't help that Mr. France had claimed he only wanted to wound the kid a little with his twelve-gauge shotgun. If that had been the case, why had he loaded the gun with double-aught shells? But Hoke didn't cross out the *address* of Mr. France. Sides had been taken in the neighborhood, and Mrs. France, also seventy-two, was going to get some harassment.

Marshall Fisher—a DOA—suicide. That was cut-and-dried, but there was going to be an inquest, and he'd have to appear. He made a check mark to watch his in box for a notice on Fisher.

There were three convenience-store killings under investigation, but no leads. Signs were posted in English and Spanish in all the convenience stores, stating that the managers were only allowed to have $35 in the cash register. But the Cuban managers were killed by Cuban gunmen for the $35. American prisons didn't frighten Marielito criminals; after Castro's, American prisons were country clubs. And when a witness to a killing was found, which was seldom, he was too scared to point out the killer.

When Hoke ran across the address, "K.P.T.—157 Ave.—6–418E," he was puzzled for a few moments. Not only was he hungry but he had a lot on his mind. There was no name, and he didn't know anyone who lived out this far in

Kendall. Then he recalled that this was Susan Waggoner's address. Inasmuch as 157th Avenue was Dade County, and not Miami Police Department territory, Hoke rarely got this far west. All of West Kendall came under Metro Police jurisdiction.

Hoke was curious about this peculiar couple, and especially the jock, although he didn't believe for a second that Susan had ordered "Junior Mendez" to break her brother's finger. She had seemed too dimwitted even to entertain the idea, but still, it wouldn't hurt anything to talk to her while he was out this way. He might pick up some information on the boyfriend. If they were college students studying for degrees in management, maybe he and Henderson should enroll in a seminary and work on doctor of divinity degrees.

THE TALL UNFINISHED buildings in Kendall Pines Terrace reminded Hoke of the Roman apartment houses he had seen in Italian neorealist movies. The Salvadoran guard on the gate explained how to get to Building Six, and Hoke took the winding road to the last parking lot, avoiding the speed bumps by going around them on the grass. He parked in a visitors' slot to avoid being towed away—as advised by the gatekeeper—and rode the elevator to the fourth floor.

Susan opened the door on the first knock, having a little difficulty with the new deadbolt lock, which was still stiff.

"I don't have much to tell you, Miss Waggoner," Hoke said. "But I was out this way, so I thought I'd drop by for a few minutes and talk to you."

Susan was wearing a black dress with hose and black pumps. She had also applied some rouge to her cheeks and wore pink lipstick. There was a string of imitation pearls around her thin neck. The dress was too big for her, and she reminded Hoke of a little girl playing dress-up in her mother's clothes.

"Would you like a beer, sergeant? Coffee?"

"No, no. Thanks, but I just had lunch."

"Lunch? It's almost five-thirty."

"An early dinner, then. I missed lunch, actually, so I had something just now at the Roseate Spoon Bill."

"I go there a lot. I like the Mexican pizza."

"I've never tried that."

"It's really good. Lots of cheese."

"I'll try it some time. Your father came in this morning, Miss Waggoner, and he claimed the two hundred dollars."

"He would."

"But we're going to hold on to the effects for a while. I was going to call the Krishnas today, but I've been busy with other things. Has your father contacted you today?"

Susan shook her head. "He won't, either. But I don't plan on going to the funeral, anyway."

"He said he was going to cremate your brother and scatter the ashes on Lake Okeechobee."

"Martin would like that. He always liked the lake."

"Your father's staying at the Royalton, downtown, if you want to call him."

"I don't."

"Where's Mendez?"

"Who?"

"Ramon. Your fiancé?"

"Oh, Junior, you mean. His name is Ramon Mendez, Junior, but he always goes by Junior. He hates to be called Ramon."

"How'd you happen to meet him?"

"We met in English class at Dade. He helped me write my haikus. I was having trouble with them."

"Haikus? What are they?"

"It's some kind of Japanese poem."

"I see. So you met at school and got engaged."

"That's right. But now we have what's called a platonic marriage."

"He lives here with you, then?"

"He should be home soon. If you want to ask questions about Junior, you should talk to him."

"What smells so good?"

85

"That's dinner. I'm cooking stuffed pork chops. I use Stove-Top dressing, shallots, and mushrooms, all smothered in brown gravy. Also, baked sweet potatoes, peas, and a tomato and cucumber and onion salad. Do you think I should make hot biscuits?"

"Does Junior like biscuits?"

"I really don't know. I've got white bread, but I think I'll fix some. Most men like hot biscuits. Would you like to stay for dinner?"

"I've already eaten. I told you. You've got a lovely apartment here, Miss Waggoner."

"Oh, I don't own it. I rent it, furnished."

"It must be rough on you, working and going to school, too."

"It isn't so bad. The work at the International Hotel isn't hard, and I don't have to work at night."

"What are you—a maid?"

"Oh, no!" Susan laughed. "Maids only get minimum wage. I get fifty dollars a trick, and split it down the middle with Pablo. I'm one of Pablo Lhosa's girls. That is, I was, but I quit. Now that we've got a platonic marriage, Junior doesn't want me to work for Pablo anymore."

"You're a hooker, then?"

"I thought you knew. You aren't going to arrest me, are you?"

"No, that isn't my department. I just work homicides. I guess I've been lucky so far. I was with the Riviera Police Department for three years, and I've been in Miami for twelve, and I've never had to work Vice. When d'you expect Junior home?"

"When he gets here. It doesn't make any nevermind to me. The pork chops are in the Crockpot, and the other stuff won't take long. The potatoes are already done. He said he'd be home at six, but he might be late."

Hoke handed her one of his cards. "Have Junior call me when he gets home tonight. It says the Eldorado Hotel in Miami Beach, but I'm reachable there. If the phone isn't

86

answered right away, tell him to let it ring. There's only one man on the desk at night, and if he's away from the desk it takes a little time to get an answer. Somebody'll answer eventually."

"All right. I'll tell him, but that doesn't mean he'll call you."

"Just tell him I've been looking through some mug books."

"Mug books?"

"He'll know what I mean." Hoke went to the door.

"Sergeant Moseley? You didn't tell daddy about the car, did you?"

Hoke shook his head. "No. He didn't ask, and I didn't volunteer."

THE TRAFFIC WAS heavy on North Kendall and heavier on Dixie, when Hoke turned toward downtown. It was after seven by the time Hoke reached LeJeune Road. He stopped for gas and made a phone call to the duty officer in Homicide, leaving a message for Sergeant Henderson to call him at home. He made another call to the morgue and learned that they did not plan to start the post-mortems on the Colombians until the next day, probably late in the afternoon. He paid for the gas, put the receipt in his notebook, and decided to go home. He could work on his report in the morning. Perhaps by then Henderson would have something from the woman's testimony.

Hoke took the MacArthur Causeway to South Beach but decided to stop for a boilermaker at Irish Mike's before going home. Mike brought him the shot of Early Times and a Miller's draft, then waited until Hoke downed the shot and took a sip of beer.

"I suppose you'll be wanting this on the tab, sergeant?"

"Yeah, and one more shot besides. I've still got enough beer."

"D'you know what your tab is?"

"No, you tell me."

"It was eighty-five bucks." Mike poured another shot into Hoke's glass. "Not countin' these two."

"I didn't know it was that much."

"That's what it is, sergeant. When it hits a hundred I'm gonna eighty-six you till you pay the whole tab. I wouldn't object to something on account right now."

"I wouldn't mind giving you something on account, Mike, but I'm a little short right now. I'll bring in fifty on payday, but don't let it run up so high again."

"I'm not the one that runs it up—you are."

Mike went into the back, and Hoke quickly downed the second shot, finished the beer, and left the bar. He was depressed enough already without being hit for an $85 bar tab. Hoke didn't drink all that much, but when he wanted a drink he hated to drink alone in his room. Fortunately, he had a bottle of El Presidente at home. This was one time he would have to keep himself company.

Hoke got into his car and drove to the Eldorado Hotel.

11

BEFORE LEAVING KENDALL Pines Terrace, Freddy had locked the pistol in the glove compartment and spread the city map of Miami out on the passenger's seat. He turned east on Kendall and took the Homestead Extension Freeway north toward the city. The traffic didn't get heavy until he turned east again on Dolphin Expressway toward the airport. By watching the overhead signs carefully, he avoided the lane that would have taken him across the causeway to Miami Beach and managed to bluff his way into the left lane that took him down to Biscayne Boulevard. He was astonished by the erratic driving on the freeway. If they drove this way in Los Angeles, he thought, most of these people would have been killed within minutes. Freddy didn't consider himself a good driver, but compared to these Miami drivers he was a professional.

On impulse, he turned into the Omni Mall and took the ramp to the third level before finding a parking space. The parking garage was color-coded as well as numbered, and he wrote *Purple 3* on his parking ticket before putting it into his hip pocket.

Using the Mendez Visa card, he bought two short-sleeve sports shirts in the County Seat, and then paid cash for a featherweight poplin suit in an Italian men's store. The suit was on sale for $350. To make the sale, however, the salesman had to get a pair of pants with a twenty-nine-inch waist from another suit to go with the size forty-two jacket. He bought two $25 neckties in another men's shop, using the Mendez card, and then a pair of cordovan tasseled loafers for $150 cash at Bally's. He returned to the TransAm and locked his purchases in the trunk. He went back into the mall and bought a stuffed baked potato at One Potato, Two—asking for the Mexican Idaho, which included butter, chili con carne, jack cheese, and tortilla chips. The chili was hot, and he drank a large Tab with lots of ice.

All he had to buy now was a box of white shirts and a present for Susan. She was not the kind of girl who had been given many presents, and she would be happy with anything he got her. She was so passive in bed that he doubted that she had ever had any tips from her clients.

In addition to its three shopping levels, the air-conditioned mall was anchored at each end with a Penney's and a Jordan Marsh department store. There was also an involved egress to the Omni Hotel. A man could get lost quickly in the Omni Mall, but not for very long because of the color-coded exits and numbers.

A portly man in a blue-and-white seersucker suit was standing in front of the store window and looking intently at the merchandise. As Freddy glanced at him, wondering what it was in the window that held his attention, a small dark man with a bushy head of curly hair bumped against the portly man, apologized, and walked on. Freddy saw the small man slip the wallet out of the heavy man's hip pocket, but the man hadn't felt a thing. Freddy trailed behind the small man, who was wearing a blue serge suit and a blue wool tie, to the escalator and watched him drop the wallet into another man's folded newspaper, *El Diario*. The pickpocket continued through the mall, and the one with the newspaper, a tall dark man with black sideburns down to and even with his mouth, took the Down escalator.

Freddy got on the escalator behind him. He followed him past Treasure Island and the carousel, and into the lowest level of the mall. The man strolled past the Unicorn Store, a T-shirt store, skirted a French sidewalk café, and then went into the men's room. Freddy waited outside the door counting to thirty, then went in. The tall man with the sideburns had the wallet in his hands. He looked up at Freddy for a moment and then back down at the wallet. Freddy grabbed his left wrist, twisted it behind his back with one motion, and then ran the man into the white-tiled wall, face-first. The man screamed something in Spanish and tried to get his right hand into his trousers pocket. Freddy jerked the left arm higher and it broke at the elbow. As the arm cracked, the man vomited and fell to his knees. Freddy kicked him behind the ear, and the man went unconscious.

Freddy picked up the wallet from the floor and stuffed it into his pocket. He searched the man on the floor. There was a pearl-handled switchblade knife in his right front pocket and a roll of bills held together with a rubber band in the left hip pocket. He found another wallet in an inside jacket pocket. Freddy stuffed these into his pockets and washed his hands. A teenager, wearing a red-billed Red Man cap, jeans, and a CLASH T-shirt, walked in and saw the man on the floor, bubbling blood from his mouth and ears, then went to the urinal.

"What's the matter with that guy?"

"Ask him," Freddy said, blotting his hands dry on a brown paper towel.

"I don't want to get involved," the teenager said, unzipping his fly.

Freddy left the men's room and took the stairwell up to Level Two. He bought a box of three white-on-white Excello shirts at Baron's. He bought a pedestal coffee cup that had *Susie* printed on the side in Old English script, and a half-pound bag of Colombian coffee. He asked the girl at the coffee shop to gift-wrap the two items together, which cost him an extra $1.50. He returned to his car and locked his new purchases into the trunk before getting into the front seat and turning on the engine and the air conditioning.

Freddy counted $322 from the portly man's stolen wallet, $809 from the tall man's wallet, and $1,200 from the tight roll of bills. In the middle of the tight roll of American money, there was an even tighter roll of 10,000 Mexican pesos. So, not counting the pesos, which he might be able to exchange later, he was $2,331 richer than when he had arrived at the Omni—minus the cash he had put out for his shopping, of course. This was absolutely the best haul Freddy had ever made in a single day. He had also picked up two new credit cards—the fat man's—a Visa and a MasterCard. The tall man with sideburns, apparently the other half of a Mexico City pickpocket team, had a green card in the name of Jaime Figueras in his wallet. This meant that he could work in Miami, but it didn't authorize him to work as a pickpocket; he would be unlikely to report his mugging to the police. If that damned kid hadn't come into the men's room, Freddy could have waited for a few minutes and made another nice haul after the short partner came down for his cut. But probably it was just as well. He had gotten in trouble before by staying too long in a men's room. Vice Squad cops pretending to be gay, and some who didn't have to pretend, hit public rest rooms all the time to top off their daily arrest quotas.

Freddy paid the parking fee to the Cuban girl at the exit and drove south on Biscayne Boulevard, planning what he would say to Pablo Lhosa at the International Hotel.

By the time he had crawled through the heavy traffic to Dupont Plaza, Freddy decided that it might be best not to see Pablo at all. Pablo knew him as Gotlieb, and by now, or at least in another day or two, the hotel would find out that it had been stiffed by a stolen credit card. Of course, the hotel would get its money, in all probability, but Pablo would have some leverage to use against him. Perhaps for the moment it would be best to do nothing. He would tell Susan not to answer her phone, and when Pablo came out to see her he could take care of him. By that time, some kind of solution would occur to him.

Freddy circled the Dupont Plaza and drove back down Biscayne to the Omni. This time he pulled into the hotel entrance. He turned over the ignition key, but not the trunk key, to the valet. He registered at the desk as Mr. and Mrs. Junior Waggoner and pocketed the room key. He counted out $1,000 in cash for a $120-a-day room and told the clerk he would return with this baggage later when he came back from the airport with his wife.

No, he told the clerk, he didn't know how long he would be staying, but to remind him when his bill got up to $900, and he would either check out then or put down some more cash as an advance. Freddy waved off the bellman and took the elevator up to his room.

He stashed the extra wallets and the pesos in the bedside table next to the king-size bed and went back down to the lobby entrance for his car. He paid for the valet parking, gave the valet a quarter, and turned off the salsa that was blaring full blast from his radio. If the valet hadn't turned on the radio he would have gotten a dollar instead of a quarter, Freddy reflected. He headed south on Biscayne again. He crossed the Miami River and drove down Brickell. He now had two nice hidey-holes, one in Kendall and another downtown in Omni. To avoid the sun and the heat, he could work the Omni Mall; the way the Omni was laid out, it was a thief's paradise. If he only robbed pickpockets, he could work for weeks without any fear of detection. Of course, there would be competition; there was bound to be in a perfect setup like that. Freddy didn't mind a little competition. As the fly said, crossing the mirror, "That's just another way of looking at it."

FREDDY PARKED ON the roof of the bus company's parking garage and spent two hours exploring the Miracle Mile in Coral Gables. The stores were owned by Americans, but they catered to Latin tastes. Women's clothing was on the garish side, with lots of ruffles and flounces. Primary colors were predominant, with very few pastels in evidence. Men's suits were gray or blue, with thin stripes in rust or coral, and the shirts and ties were like those Freddy remembered from Santa Anita, when he used to spend his afternoons at the track. Except for the incredible cleanliness, the Coral Gables shopping street reminded Freddy of East Los Angeles, although East LA had never been this prosperous.

In a sporting goods store, Freddy bought three All-American Official Frisbees, charging them to the Mendez credit card. He went back to the roof of the parking garage, took the Frisbees out of the paper sack, and ripped off their plastic wrappings. He then sailed them, one at a time, across the street, and over a lower roof, watching them land and skitter in the heavy traffic on LeJeune Road. Two cellmates at San Quentin had owned a Frisbee, and Freddy had often watched them throw it back and forth to each other in the yard. They would laugh when they caught it, and they would laugh even harder when one of them failed to catch it. Freddy had always wanted to toss it himself, but the two cons never let anyone else into their game, and of course, no one ever asked them for a turn. But throwing the three Frisbees hadn't been much fun; perhaps you needed a partner to aim at.

FREDDY GOT LOST trying to get through the complex of the University of Miami, gave up, and finally drove around the school before he could find Miller Road. He got back to Kendall Pines Terrace at six-thirty.

Freddy dumped his packages on the couch, handed Susan her gift-wrapped present, and checked the new deadbolt lock on the front door. He accepted the girlish kiss she planted on his cheek for the gift and told her to buy some 3-in-One Oil the next time she went to the store. She told Freddy about Sergeant Moseley's visit and handed him the detective's card. Freddy made her repeat word for word everything that had been said.

"Did he say 'local' mug shots, or 'wanted' mug shots?"

"He just said mug books. He said you'd know what he meant."

"You shouldn't've told him you worked for Pablo. That wasn't too bright."

"I thought he knew."

"The best thing to say to a cop is nothing. Remember that. Did Pablo call you?"

"No. Well, he might have. There were two phone calls, but I didn't answer the phone. If it was Pablo, I knew I wouldn't know what to say, and if it was you, you would've said you'd call and you didn't."

"At least you did something right. Get your purse. I'm going over to Miami Beach and see the cop."

"What about dinner? Everything's ready."

"We'll take it with us."

In the closet there was a large cardboard box filled with Martin's fishing gear. Freddy dumped it out, and Susan packed the box with the Crockpot and the rest of the items on her menu. Working hurriedly, she was soon ready to go, and she had to wait for Freddy to shower and change into his new suit and Bally loafers. The .38 made a bulge in Freddy's jacket pocket, but he didn't like to carry a pistol in his waistband because of an accident a friend of his had once in San Diego.

As the blacks used to say in the yard at Quentin when they wanted to get even with a bully, Freddy was "going to pull that fucker's teeth, man!"

12

WHEN HOKE WALKED into the lobby of the Eldorado Hotel, Old Man Zuckerman jumped up from his faded brocade chair by the entrance and handed him a neatly folded paper napkin. Hoke thanked the old man and put the napkin in his pocket. Mr. Zuckerman smiled toothlessly and sat back down in his chair. Mr. Zuckerman was well into his eighties, and his "job" was to give every person who entered the hotel a paper napkin, and he forced it on visitors and residents alike, including Mr. Howard Bennett, the owner-manager, every time they came in. Hoke figured that this job that Mr. Zuckerman had invented for himself helped to keep the old follow alive. And Old Man Zuckerman had an endless supply of paper napkins, because he helped himself to all he would need when he ate his meals at Gold's Deli down the street.

The Eldorado Hotel was a deteriorating art-deco hotel that was on the verge of being condemned. It was scheduled to be torn down if Redevelopment came to South Miami Beach. But Redevelopment had been in the planning stage for almost ten years now, and nothing was ever done. Because of the building moratorium on South Beach the owners weren't repairing anything they didn't positively have to take care of, except for meeting the most minimal requirements for fire and safety. By acting as an unpaid hotel security officer when he was off duty, Hoke got a free room, but he had been considering moving out for several months.

His problem was money. Every other paycheck went to his ex-wife in Vero Beach, and he had to live on the other half. After term life insurance payments, car insurance, retirement payments, and union dues, he had to live on less than $12,000 a year. With a free room and with his battered Le Mans paid for, that should have been enough—or more than enough—but there had been his own hospital bills, plus a new and enormous bill for his two daughters' orthodontist. He had ripped up the bill from the orthodontist, but then Patsy, his ex-wife, had threatened to take him to court. Part of the divorce settlement was that he would pay for the girls' medical expenses. Straightening teeth, in Hoke's opinion, came under beautification, and was not a necessary medical expense. But to avoid going to court, he had finally sent the orthodontist a check for $50 and told him he would try to make some regular payments on the $1,800 bill.

The shabby lobby was depressing. Eight old ladies, all members of the Eldorado Hotel TV Club, sat in a silent half-circle, watching a television set that was bolted and locked to the wall. When Hoke looked across the room, four Marielitos, playing dominoes at a corner table, got respectfully to their feet, nodded shyly at him, and sat down again when he acknowledged their greeting with a wave of his right arm. On his way to the desk Hoke took a look at the TV screen and saw a green snake eat a red frog. Education Night. He checked his mailbox (Eddie Cohen wasn't at the desk) and decided that tonight he would only make perfunctory rounds.

On the way to his room on the eighth floor, he stopped the elevator at each floor, looked up and down the halls without getting out, and then went on. On the fifth floor, however, he saw Mrs. Friedman wandering around in her nightgown. He locked the elevator and led the old lady back to her room before going up to six. She often got confused, and when she happened to leave her room she could never remember her room number. Rumor had it that the meals-on-wheels program was either going to be reduced or cut out altogether, and when that happened, he didn't know what Mrs. Friedman would do for sustenance. Even when her social security check came in, she wouldn't be able to find her way down to Gold's Deli and back.

It was depressing to think about Mrs. Friedman, but it had been even more depressing to find out that Susan Waggoner was a whore. Even Hoke wouldn't have figured that in a hundred years. Bill Henderson, who had worked Vice for three years, probably could have taken one look at Susan and known, but Hoke hadn't suspected it. Hell, Hoke's fourteen-year-old daughter was built better and sexier looking than Susan.

And then there had been that dead baby—and the maid. The kid probably couldn't talk in sentences yet, and the maid couldn't have been more than nineteen or twenty. He didn't mourn the two Colombians. They were men in their early thirties, and whatever it was that they had done to be killed for, they had done it in their maturity. The maid, if she had been hired locally, might be a lead, but he suspected that she had been brought along from Colombia to take care of the baby.

Any way he looked at it, it was a rotten business.

Instead of going to his room, Hoke took the stairs from the eighth floor to the roof. The only good thing about the Eldorado Hotel was the view from the roof. He lit a cigarette and looked across Biscayne Bay at Miami. The white uneven buildings looked like teeth, but at this distance it was a white smile. There was even a gum-colored sunset above the skyline, and in the northwest above the Everglades there was a stack-up of black clouds that looked like thousand-dollar poker chips. It was raining in the 'Glades, and perhaps enough rain would be left to reach the city and cool it off a little during the night. Hoke finished his cigarette and tossed it off the parapet into the swimming pool behind the hotel. The pool, a small one, had been filled with sand. Without water, no one could use it, but Mr. Bennett saved money on maintenance costs with a pool full of sand. There was a lot of trash scattered over the surface. Hoke decided to put in his report that the trash was a fire hazard so that Mr. Bennett would have to have it cleaned up.

Hoke unlocked the door to his room and switched on the light by the door. The small room was stifling and smelled of dirty sheets, unwashed socks and underwear, bay rum, and stale tobacco smoke. Howard Bennett, the cheapskate owner-manager, had invaded Hoke's room during his absence and pulled the plug on Hoke's window air conditioner to save energy costs. Hoke plugged in the air conditioner and turned it up to High.

He took off his leisure suit jacket, his gun, his handcuffs, and sap, and tossed the equipment on the top of his cluttered dresser. He switched on his small black-and-white Sony and poured two inches of El Presidente brandy into his tooth glass. "Family Feud" was on the tube, and for the hundredth time Hoke wondered about the definition of *family* in America. There were five family members on both teams, but no mothers or fathers. Instead, there were various uncles and cousins and spouses of the cousins, plus one teenage kid who bore no resemblance to either family and had probably been borrowed from neighbors for the program.

There was a knock on the door. Hoke sighed and hid the glass of brandy behind a photograph of his two daughters on the dresser. The last time he had had a visitor knocking on his door it had been Mrs. Goldberg, from 409. Her ex-husband, she told him, had sneaked into her room while she was watching television in the lobby and had stolen her pearl-handled hairbrush, the hairbrush that had belonged to her mother. Hoke had gone down to 409 with her and found the hairbrush in the bottom drawer of Mrs. Goldberg's dresser.

"He must've hidden it there," she said.

Later on, when Hoke had mentioned the incident to Mr. Bennett, the manager had laughed and told Hoke that Mrs. Goldberg had been a widow for fifteen years.

Hoke reached for the doorknob.

13

SUSAN DROVE. THE traffic was all coming their way, so she made good time as she drove east on Killian to Old Cutler, then turned north to drive through Coconut Grove. The tropical foliage was thick and green on Old Cutler, and after they passed Fairchild Gardens, the air roots from the overhanging tree branches frequently whipped the roof of the car.

Susan rejoined South Dixie beyond Vizcaya, then took Brickell Avenue to Biscayne Boulevard. She took the toll-free MacArthur Causeway to South Beach. The Eldorado Hotel was near Joe's Stone Crab Restaurant, and because Susan knew where the restaurant was she had no trouble finding the old hotel on the bay.

"Wait in the car," Freddy told her, after she parked in the small lot beside the hotel.

"How long?"

"For as long as it takes me. If he's home, it won't take long. If he isn't home, I'll have to wait in his room till he gets there. So just sit here and wait."

"Can I play the radio?"

"No. It might attract attention. Stop asking dumb questions."

Freddy went into the lobby, and Old Man Zuckerman tottered over to him and handed him a napkin. Freddy nodded his thanks, and the old man went back to his chair and fell into a half-doze. There were four men playing dominoes in the corner of the lobby and some old ladies watching TV at the other end. The battered card table, where the Latins were playing, was lighted by a 1930s wrought-iron bridge lamp with a rose shade and tarnished gold tassels. The men all wore T-shirts and jeans, none of them clean. One man had a machete scar running from the top of his head down his left cheek, ending beneath his chin. All four men had blackish homemade tattoos on the backs of their hands and arms.

Freddy walked to the table, and the conversation stopped.

"Sergeant Moseley's room?" Freddy handed $10 to the man with the scar.

"Top floor." He pointed his finger at the ceiling. "Eight-Oh-Nine. *Gracias.*"

"A *casa?*"

The man ignored the question, pursed his lips, and studied his dominoes. Freddy grabbed the man's wrist, squeezed it, and took the $10 bill out of his paralyzed fingers.

" *Sí, señor,*" the man said. "A *casa.*"

"*Un hombre duro,*" Freddy said. He wadded the ten into the man's palm and closed his fingers on it.

"*¡Despotico!*" The scar-faced man nodded, and the other three Cubans laughed. Freddy crossed the dim lobby to the elevators.

Outside 809, Freddy took out his pistol, knocked on the door, and pressed his back against the wall. Hoke Moseley opened the door, saw no one, and took a step forward. Freddy, with a sweeping motion of the gun, caught Hoke on the side of the jaw. As Hoke fell sideways, Freddy had time for another backhand blow, and Hoke's false teeth flew out of his mouth and bounced on the dusty hall carpet. Freddy put the teeth into his jacket pocket and dragged the unconscious body inside the room. After closing the door, he kicked the supine man in the jaw with the point of his shoe. The jaw cracked audibly, and blood poured from Hoke's nose and mouth.

After taking off his jacket, Freddy sat on the edge of the unmade bed. He needed to cool off for a minute or so. His shirt was already drenched with sweat, and he didn't want it to darken his new suit jacket. The air conditioner in the window labored away, but it produced more noise than cold air. In the humidity, the slightest exercise provoked a good deal of perspiration. In California, Freddy would have had to work out for at least a half-hour to build up such a sweat. It was like breathing through a wet bath towel.

The room was grungy. Here was a pig, Freddy thought, who actually lived like a pig. Aluminum foil covered the sliding glass door that opened onto the tiny balcony. The foil was there to reflect the heat away from the room in the afternoons, but it hadn't helped much. The dirty beige carpet was ringed and spotted with coffee and other food spills. The sheets on the three-quarter-size bed were dirty, and there was a pile of unwashed laundry in the corner next to an overflowing wastebasket.

There were two police uniforms in heavy plastic garment bags in the closet, along with a black suit and two poplin leisure suits. There were a half-dozen clean short-sleeve sports shirts on hangers, one white dress shirt, and three neckties.

In the bottom drawer of the dresser there was a one-ring hot plate, a small saucepan, a tablespoon, a knife, a fork, three cans of Chunky Turkey Soup with noodles, and a box of Krispy saltines. There was a half-loaf of rye bread, four eggs in a brown carton, a jar of instant coffee, and a bottle of Tabasco sauce. The other dresser drawers contained papers neatly filed away in cardboard folders, Fruit of the Loom underwear, and black lisle socks. There were several

T-shirts, two pairs of ragged khaki gym shorts, and a pair of blue-and-red running shoes. The cop didn't have another pair of black dress shoes, except for the pair he was wearing. Of course, Freddy thought, he might have more shoes and clothes in his locker at the police station.

The detective, in any event, was living incredibly cheap, and Freddy couldn't understand it. On top of the man's dresser was a ticket to a lot of money: a badge and an ID in a worn leather holder, a holstered .38 police special, a sap, and handcuffs. Freddy searched Hoke's pockets. He found keys, a wallet, a package of Kools, Dupont Plaza Hotel paper matches, and eighty cents in change. There were $18 in the wallet, several business cards with notes on them, and one MasterCard. There were also two small photos in the wallet, older versions of the two young girls in the framed photo on the dresser. The detective's notebook was in his leisure jacket. Freddy flipped through it idly but could make out nothing intelligible from the shorthand Hoke used in the notebook.

Freddy sat on the edge of the bed again and tapped the black leather sap gently into the palm of his other hand. The light blow stung. The tapered sap, eight inches long, with a wrist loop at one end, was filled with buckshot. Once, in Santa Barbara, a cop had slapped Freddy on the leg with one almost like this one. There had been no reason to hit Freddy with the blackjack; Freddy had been handcuffed at the time and was sitting quietly in a straight-backed chair. The cop had tapped him because he had wanted to tap him. The pain had been excruciating. His entire leg had gone numb, and unbidden tears had burned his eyes.

Still seated, Freddy reached out, and slapped the sap sharply against the top of Hoke's right leg. Hoke groaned, and made scrabbling motions with his fingers on the frayed carpet. Freddy shrugged. Hitting the unconscious man had given him no pleasure; he still didn't know why the cop in Santa Barbara had tapped him with the sap. Policemen undoubtedly had some kind of inborn perverted streak that normal men like himself didn't have.

Freddy got a brown paper sack from the closet and dropped the holstered .38, the badge, and ID holder into it, along with the sap. He now possessed a cop's license to steal, and the equipment to go with it. He added the handcuffs to the sack and put Hoke's $18 on top of the dresser. He then put five $20 bills on top of the $18; it would help to confuse the pig even more when he woke up.

Freddy closed the door, which locked behind him, took the elevator down, and left the lobby by the side terrace French windows to avoid being seen by the domino players and the old ladies. The players could identify him, he knew, but four Latins with homemade prison tattoos wouldn't volunteer any information about an injured cop. Not unless, Freddy grinned, someone slipped them ten bucks or so—and investigating officers didn't give out any free money for information.

Freddy told Susan to take the Venetian Causeway back to the Omni Hotel in Miami. When they reached DiLido Island, he told her to stop on the other side of the island by the bridge. When she stopped the car, he got out and threw the teeth in the bay. He climbed into the front seat again.

"What did you throw away?" Susan said.

"None of your business. If you need to know, I would've told you. How many times do I have to tell you not to ask questions?"

"I'm sorry," Susan said. "I forgot."

They turned the car over to valet parking, and when Freddy showed his room key to the doorman, a bellman came out with a cart and brought Susan's prepared dinner up to their room. Freddy dialed room service and ordered a bottle of champagne, a pot of coffee, and table service for two. They ate the stuffed pork chops and still-warm sweet potatoes by candlelight in the handsomely appointed room, with a magnificent view of Biscayne Bay and the Miami Beach skyline.

Freddy complimented Susan on the pork chops and biscuits, even though they were cold.

If Susan was still curious, she kept her questions to herself.

14

WHEN HOKE MOVED his right leg it hurt more than his jaw, but at least he could move it. The top of his head seemed to rise and fall eerily with each breath. His head was immobilized by two pillows so that he could not move it more than an inch or two to either side. His wrists were tied loosely to the bedrails with gauze, which prevented him from feeling his face or poking at the bandages. There were tubs and racks with bottles in each side of his bed, and clear fluids dripped into both arms. Perhaps that was why his arms were restrained.

Hoke's lower face was completely numb. From his position on the bed, with his head raised slightly, all he could see was a gray steel contraption on the wall. He wondered vaguely what it was, but it was two more days before he found out that the steel frame was a bracket for the television set, and that if he signed a piece of paper he could have a TV set brought in so he could watch the tube instead of the bracket.

By the end of the first week, when Hoke could sit up and go to the bathroom without help, he considered ordering the TV set, but he never did. As he recalled, there were too many commercials about food, in color, on TV, and he knew that the commercials would make him hungrier than he was already. Sometimes, when he closed his eyes, he could visualize the Burger King double cheeseburger with the bacon sizzling on top. He was hungry all the time.

There were four beds in the ward, but Hoke was the only occupant. This was a special oral surgeon's ward in St. Mary's Hospital in Miami Shores, and it was used exclusively by dentists and oral surgeons who had patients with special problems. Except for a fourteen-year-old Jewish American Prince whose mother had him checked in overnight to have a back tooth extracted, Hoke had the small ward to himself throughout his stay. Hoke disliked the room, hated the hospital, and detested the gay male nurse, a Canary Islander who took an unseemly pleasure in giving Hoke an enema.

Hoke had been operated on by an oral surgeon named Murray Goldstein, and by his own dentist of several years standing, Dr. David Rubin. Dr. Rubin professed sympathy for Hoke, but he had never forgiven him for having Doc Evans pull his teeth out in the morgue. Still, he seemed elated by the fact that Hoke's damaged jaw would be able to support a new set of false teeth. But the new teeth had to be held off until Hoke's jaw had healed and all of the bone splinters came out. Meanwhile, his mandible was immobilized, wired here and there, and he drank his meals through a glass straw. The bruise on top of his right leg was the size and shape of a football, and he limped for several days after he was up and into his bedside chair.

While he was still punchy from the drugs and unable to talk, Red Farris visited him and brought Louise along. He could remember Red's droopy red mustache hanging over him, and Louise's white face and rain-dark hair hovering ghostily in the doorway. He couldn't remember what Red Farris had said, but Red had left a note with his presents, all of which Hoke found later in his bedside table. There was a bottle of Smirnoff vodka and a one-pound package of fudge wrapped in gold paper with the note:

Use the vodka for mouthwash. It's breathless. Louise made you some fudge. When I get settled in Sebring, you can come up for recuperation and we'll go dove hunting.

Take care.
"Red"

When Farris didn't come back later, after Hoke could have visitors, Hoke assumed that he had left for Sebring. But Hoke knew that he would never go dove hunting with Red Farris; once a man left Miami, that was the end of it, and Red knew it as well as he did.

Although his jaw was still wired and he could talk only with difficulty, Hoke was glad to see Bill Henderson. Bill told Hoke that the case of the four dead Colombians had been solved.

Henderson had borrowed a skycap's uniform and cap, put them on one of his black detectives, and had him falsely finger the Colombian woman as the person in a purple Cadillac who had dropped off two men at the Miami International Airport. Confronted by this direct, if false, identification, she had broken down. The child, as it turned out, was the maid's, not her own, and the child was not supposed to be killed. She was upset about that, which helped to make up her mind, too. The killers were back safely in Cartagena and would never be extradited. But at least their names were known now, so it was unlikely that the same pair would be used in Miami for more assassinations.

"I knew she was in on it for sure, Hoke, when you told me there were no packages in the trunk. The woman had nine hundred bucks in her purse, and there is no way that a woman could shop for two hours with that kind of money and not buy something."

Henderson shrugged. "But she hasn't been arraigned yet. I've got a hunch that they'll set bail for a hundred thousand

and let her skip back to Colombia. That's what usually happens."

Hoke nodded, and made a circle with his thumb and forefinger. Henderson pulled his chair closer to the bed.

"You got any idea who did this to you, Hoke?"

"Uh-uh." Hoke rolled his head back and forth on the pillow.

"Got *any* ideas?"

Hoke nodded and then shrugged. He was tired, and he wanted Henderson to leave.

"I talked some to Eddie Cohen, the old fart on the desk, and he says he didn't see any strangers in the hotel. The manager questioned some of the old ladies who sit around the TV set in the lobby, and they didn't notice anyone either."

Henderson got up, and walked to the window. He looked down into the parking lot. "I—ah—I checked your room, Hoke, and I really don't think you should be living in a crummy place like that. All those social security types and Marielitos—it's depressing as shit, Hoke. When you get out of here, you'll have to recuperate for a couple of weeks. I can put you up at my house. We can put a cot out in the Florida room, and Marie'll look after you."

"No dice, Bill." Hoke closed his eyes. After a few seconds, Henderson tapped him on the shoulder.

"Well, think about it anyway, old sport. I'd better get outta here and let you get some rest. If you need anything, let me know."

After Henderson left, Hoke found the carton of Kools and the new Bic lighter his partner had left in a paper sack on the floor beside his bed. Hoke had lost his desire to smoke; if he was lucky, maybe the desire wouldn't return.

Captain Willie Brownley was Hoke's third visitor. The captain had been there to look in on him a couple of times before. Brownley was black, and it was the first time Hoke had seen the Homicide chief in civilian clothes. He always wore his uniform in the office, complete with buttoned-up jacket. Now he wore a pink Golden Bear knitted shirt, mauve corduroy jeans, a white belt, and white shoes. With his gold-rimmed glasses, Brownley looked more like a Liberty City dentist than a police captain. Hoke had known Brownley for ten years, and at one time had worked for Brownley when he commanded the Traffic Division. Although Brownley had little aptitude for Homicide work, he had been placed in charge of that division so that he could eventually be promoted to major. The black caucus in the union had been demanding a black major for several years, and Brownley was being groomed.

Brownley opened his briefcase on the bed and handed Hoke a one-pound box of fudge that had been wrapped in gold paper and tied with a flexible gold string.

"My wife made some fudge for you, Hoke," he said. "And if you can't eat it now, you'll be able to later. And the boys asked me to bring you this card." He handed Hoke a Hallmark get-well card that had been signed by forty of the forty-seven members of the Homicide division, including Captain Brownley.

Without thinking, Hoke had counted the signatures and was wondering why the other seven hadn't signed. Then he felt ashamed of himself. There were a hundred reasons— sickness, leave, shift changes—why they all couldn't sign the card.

"For a while there," Captain Brownley said, "we were worried about you, but Dr. Goldstein said you're going to be fine. The only immediate problem is to take care of the paperwork on your lost gun and shield. I hate to lay it on you, Hoke, but we've got to protect you.

"I've brought the forms along and a legal pad, and you can take care of the paperwork now. It's been about six years since a Homicide cop lost his shield and gun, but the big question to answer in your case is why you were living in Miami Beach instead of Miami in the first place. I knew you were living in the Eldorado, and I okayed it as a temporary residence. But you've been there for almost a year now, and that puts both of us in a spot. As you know, all Miami cops are supposed to live in Miami—"

"I know at least a dozen who don't—"

"I know more than that, Hoke, including a city commissioner who commutes down here from Boca Raton. But he has an official address in Miami to beat the system, and we can do the same. Henderson told me your official address is his house, so put that down on the forms."

"There's no way I can live with Henderson and his wife."

"I'm not asking you to; all I want you to do is use his address on the forms so we can cover our ass. First, fill out the Victim's Report so I can get a cop from Robbery to begin an investigation. Next, you've got to send me a red-liner memo explaining the circumstances, and third, you need to fill in this Lost and Damaged Equipment form. As soon as you've done this, I'll get the badge and gun numbers into the computer. Just write the info on the yellow pad and sign the forms. I can have them typed at the station. It's a legitimate loss, so the city'll replace your gun and badge at no cost to you, and that's about it. I'll do everything I can to prevent an investigation of why you were living in the Eldorado instead of Miami."

"That rule's never enforced," Hoke said. "There're guys with condos in Hialeah and Kendall, captain."

"Nothing is enforced until something happens. Then it's a different story. A black division chief isn't allowed to make any mistakes. I gave you temporary permission to live on the Beach, and you stayed for a year. It's my mistake for not following up on you, because now there's a thief running around Dade County with your gun and buzzer. If he ever realizes the kind of power that represents, the department'll be in a lot of trouble."

Hoke shrugged and reached for the ball point pen. "When do you want all this info?"

"Why don't you do it now? I'll go down to the cafeteria downstairs and get a sandwich and some coffee. I want to

112

get that info into the computer." Brownley turned in the doorway. "You want anything? Coffee?"

Hoke shook his head, and pulled his wheeled tray closer to the bed.

"Okay, then, Hoke, I'll be back in an hour. Don't let the nurse or no one else touch my briefcase."

Hoke filled in the forms, and wrote the red-liner memo. Although it was possible for a cop to be suspended with pay for not living in Miami, the rule was never enforced, and he thought Brownley was a little paranoid about it. But then, Brownley wanted that promotion, and Hoke didn't want to jeopardize it. Perhaps he would, after all, have to move away from the Eldorado—but he sure as hell wouldn't move in with Henderson. Hoke didn't like Marie Henderson, and he liked Henderson's kids even less.

When Captain Brownley returned for the forms, Hoke told him to thank his wife for the fudge.

"I'll tell her. D'you want any visitors, Hoke?"

"I'd rather not, captain. I look like hell, and it hurts me to talk."

"Okay, I'll pass the word, but I'll be back ex officio. One other thing, Hoke, you'll have a new partner when you come back to duty. I let Henderson stay with you when he was promoted to sergeant because you guys work well together, but things've changed lately. I'm getting five new investigators, all Cubans, all bilingual, and neither you nor Henderson speak Spanish. I've put Lopez with Henderson, and you'll have a bilingual partner when you get back. Even if you and Henderson were bilingual, I'd have to break you up. I'm too short on experienced people to let two sergeants work together any longer."

"I'm not surprised," Hoke said. "Did you know that Red Farris resigned?"

"In Robbery?"

"Yeah, and he had ten years in. He was in Homicide before you came in as chief."

"I knew Red. I didn't know him well, but I knew him

113

enough to talk to him. He was a good man. We're losing too many good people, Hoke."

WITH HIS MEMORY refreshed by the reports he had just written, Hoke went over again in his mind what had happened. There had been a knock on the door. Was it timid or imperious? Was it three raps or two? He couldn't remember. Masculine or feminine—he felt, somehow, that it was feminine, but he wasn't sure. His response had been so automatic, it was as if he had known the caller. He had hidden his drink behind the photograph of his two daughters. Why? He was entitled, for Christ's sake, to have a drink in his own room and to answer his door with a drink in his hand. It wasn't the Dominican maid, he knew her timid, tentative knock; and it wasn't Mr. Bennett. If that bastard Bennett had wanted to clobber him, he would have gypped the assailant on the fee, and the job wouldn't have been so thorough.

That left the Marielitos, but Hoke felt that the resident Cubans could be eliminated. When Hoke had first moved into the Eldorado, the refugees had been a continual problem. There had been twenty of them all in one room, and Mr. Bennett had charged them three bucks a night to sleep on mattresses on the floor. They got drunk, they fought, they were loud, and they brought women in, terrifying the Jewish retirees who lived there on social security. Hoke had shaken down their room a couple of times and picked up a .32 pistol (no one had claimed it or knew how it got there) and three knives. Finally, when Reagan took away their $115-a-month government checks, the refugees without jobs had moved out, unable to pay the three bucks a night. Hoke had then persuaded Mr. Bennett to get rid of the worst offenders, so now there were only five or six Marielitos left, and they all had jobs of some kind. Hoke figured they all liked him. He would pass out a dollar now and then—to wash his car or to bring him a sandwich from Gold's Deli. So if his attacker was a Marielito, it had to be one that he had evicted. But the attack wasn't in the Latin manner. When a Latin wanted revenge, he also wanted you to know all about it, and he would tell you at great length precisely what he was going to do to you and why before he got around to doing it.

Hoke knew that he had his share of enemies. What policeman hasn't? He had put his quota of people away, and the parole board released them faster than they were incarcerated. There were bound to be a few who might keep their promise to get him when they were released. On the other hand, a stretch in prison had a way of cooling people off. There was ample time for reflection in prison, and time, if it didn't eliminate animosity, at least ameliorated it. Hoke, like most men, considered himself a good guy. He couldn't conceive how anyone who knew him could attack him in such a cruel, impersonal way.

Hoke came to the conclusion that he had been mistaken for someone else, and the incident was some kind of crazy mixup.

He also thought it was peculiar that both boxes of fudge, the one from Louise and the one from Captain Brownley, had been wrapped in the same gold paper and tied with the same kind of flexible gold string. A few days later, when he was limping around the hospital corridors, just to get out of his room, he went into the hospital gift shop. There was a pyramid of fudge on the counter, each pound wrapped in gold paper. Hoke looked at a box and saw the sticker on the bottom: *Gray Lady Fudge—$4.95*.

15

FREDDY HAD ALWAYS been a light sleeper, but noise had seldom interrupted his sleep. In prison, he could sleep soundly while two men in the same cell argued at the top of their voices, and with bars clanging throughout the block. But if there was a change in the pattern of the usual noises he would awake immediately, as alert as an animal, until he discovered what had disturbed the pattern. He could then drop back to sleep as easily as he had awakened.

He awoke now, at four-thirty A.M., but heard nothing except the gentle hissing of the cold air from the wall ducts. Susan, her left thumb in her mouth, slept soundlessly beside him, naked except for the sheet they had pulled waist-high over themselves. There was a gentle flurry in Freddy's stomach, as though mice were scrambling around inside. His mouth was dry, and despite the air conditioning, there was a light film of perspiration on his forehead. His right leg began to jerk involuntarily, and it took him a moment or two to control the tic. He threw off the sheet and sat on the edge of the bed. To his surprise, he was a little dizzy. He poured a glass of water from the bedside carafe and ate the piece of chocolate that the maid had left on his pillow when she had turned down the bedcovers.

Freddy was having an anxiety attack, but because it was his first, he didn't know what was happening. He picked up his watch and watched the second hand sweep around as he took his pulse. He found the rate of seventy disturbing; as a rule, his pulse was a steady fifty-five. He went to the dresser, picked up Hoke's .38 police special, cocked it, and checked both closets and the bathroom. No one. He lowered the hammer carefully and replaced the weapon in the holster. He wanted to smoke a cigarette. All he had to do was to pick up the phone and he could have a carton in the room within minutes, but he didn't reach for the telephone. People in hell, he thought, want piña coladas, too. Their problem is that they can't have them. My problem is that I can have everything and anything I want, but what do I want?

He didn't want anything, including the cigarette he had thought he wanted. What did he want? Nothing. In prison he had made mental lists of all kinds of things he would get when he was released, ranging from milk shakes to powder blue Caddy convertibles. But he didn't like milk shakes because of the furry aftertaste, and a convertible in Florida would be too uncomfortably hot—unless he kept the top up and the air conditioning going full blast. So who would want a convertible?

What he needed was a purpose, and then, after he had the purpose, he would need a plan.

Freddy pulled Susan into a sitting position. "Are you awake, Susie?"

"I think so."

"Then open your eyes."

"I'm sleepy."

Freddy poured a glass of water and splashed some water into Susan's face. She rubbed her puffy eyes and blinked. "I'm awake."

"Tell me again," he said, "about the Burger King franchise."

"What?"

"The Burger King franchise. You and your brother, remember? How does it work? How much money do you need, and why do you want one?"

"It wasn't my idea, it was Marty's. What you need, he said, is about fifty thousand dollars. Then you borrow another fifty thousand from the bank and go to the Burger King people. They tell you what's available, and you buy it or lease it and run it by their rules. Marty wanted to build one up in Okeechobee. He even had the location picked out."

"But why did he want it? What was his purpose?"

"To make a living, that's all. You hire school kids real cheap, and you make a nice profit. All you have to do, as the manager, is hang around all the time, see that the place is clean, and count your money. When you pay back the bank loan, everything else you make from then on is gravy."

"What was your part supposed to be in all this?"

"Well, he said we'd split up the work, so that one of us would be there at all times. Otherwise, these kids who work for next to nothing will steal you blind. So if he was there days and I was there nights, we could prevent that."

"Is that what you wanted?"

"I don't know. It seemed like such a long way off, I didn't think much about it. Marty liked to talk about it, though. I guess I didn't care. It would be something to do, I guess. I don't know."

"Well, I think it's stupid. I can't see any point to hanging around a Burger King all day, no matter how much money you make. Don't you know why it's stupid?"

"I never thought too much about it."

"I'll tell you why. Your life would depend on the random desires of people who wanted a hamburger. So you can just forget about Burger King."

"Okay. Can I go back to sleep now?"

"Yeah. I'm going out for a while. Don't let anyone in while I'm gone. Do you want anything while I'm out?"

"Uh-uh . . ." She was asleep.

FREDDY, CARRYING HOKE'S sap and handcuffs in his jacket pocket and the holstered pistol clipped to his belt in the back, and with the badge and ID case in his right trousers pocket, left the deserted lobby. He walked down Biscayne toward Sammy's, which was open twenty-four hours. The predawn air was damp, cooler this time of morning, and there was a taste of salt in the air from the bay.

At the corner, a tall black whore at the curb clawed at his arm with long black fingers.

"Lookin' for some fun?" she said.

Freddy showed her his badge. "Call it a night."

"Yes, sir." She crossed the street on the yellow light and walked swiftly away, her high heels clattering in the dark.

Freddy continued on to Sammy's, went into the clean, well-lighted restaurant, and took a corner booth. Power, he thought. Without the badge, he would have had an argument, and it would have been difficult to get rid of the whore unless he had decided to kick her in the ass. And that could have, might have, caused him some trouble. It was trouble he could handle but a hassle all the same. With the badge, it was so easy . . .

A rangy red-haired waitress came over to take his order.

"Coffee. Is that okay, or do I have to order something with it?"

"Most people do, but you don't have to."

"Okay, And pie, then."

"What kind?"

"I'm not going to eat it, so what difference does it make?"

"Yes, sir."

Freddy didn't want the coffee, either. But the long walk in the cool air had allayed his anxiety somewhat, and he began to work out a plan that would lead to a purpose. What he needed to do, he decided, was to get organized and to start over. The haiku about the frog coming to Miami and making a splash of some kind made a lot of sense. Alone, with this new city and a new chance, he could do something or other if he could only figure out what it was he was meant to do. What he wanted to do was to dump Susan, but he realized that he was now stuck with her. He had, strictly by accident, caused the death of her stupid brother. The fact that it was her brother's fault and not his didn't make any difference. Without anyone else to look after her now, she had become Freddy's responsibility. She would get no help from her father, that was a certainty. So now it was up to him. His first idea, about buying her a Burger King franchise, was out. She had no real interest in the idea, and she wouldn't be capable of running a place like that if she had one. Her dumb brother, in all probability, wouldn't have been able to run one either.

Freddy sipped his black coffee and counted the pecan halves on top of the piece of pie the redhead had brought with the coffee. The pie was warm and smelled good, but he had eaten one hell of a dinner. He wasn't hungry . . .

A black man wearing a Raiders fedora walked into the restaurant carrying a knife. He grabbed the red-haired waitress's wrist and twisted her arm into a half-nelson. She squealed and he put the point of the knife into her neck a quarter of an inch, just far enough to draw a trickle of blood, and told her to open the register.

There were two patrons in the restaurant besides Freddy, and they sat paralyzed at the counter. They were middle-aged Canadian tourists, getting an early breakfast before a drive to the Keys. The robber apparently hadn't noticed Freddy in the corner booth, or else he wasn't concerned about him. His concentration was on the waitress and the money in the till when Freddy shot him in the left kneecap. The report of the .38 was loud, but the man's scream was piercing enough to make the Canadians shudder. He dropped the waitress's arm and his knife, then fell, still screaming, to the floor. Freddy stopped the screaming in mid-shrill when he tapped him behind his right ear with the heavy leather sap.

Freddy flashed his badge. "It's okay, dear," he said to the waitress. "I'm a police officer." He held up the badge so the middle-aged couple at the counter could see it. Freddy smiled. "Police. Go ahead and finish your breakfast."

The waitress sat at the counter, put her head down on her crossed arms, and began to cry. Freddy took the billfold from the unconscious man's hip pocket and dropped it into his own jacket pocket with the handcuffs. He took out the handcuffs, decided he didn't need to use them, and then told the middle-aged couple to stay where they were while he made a call for an ambulance from the radio in his police car. They both nodded, still too numb to reply.

Freddy put a dollar bill under his coffee cup at his booth, left the restaurant, and walked back to the Omni Hotel. As he entered the lobby, he heard the police siren as the panda car hurtled down Biscayne toward Sammy's. He sat in a red leather chair in the lobby and took out the robber's billfold. Eighty dollars. There were three driver's licenses in the billfold, all with different names but with the same picture. Freddy had no use for the licenses or the billfold, but he could always use another eighty dollars. He dropped the billfold into a potted plant and took the elevator up to his room. He had an idea now, on how to take care of Pablo Lhosa.

FREDDY SHOOK SUSAN awake, told her to take a shower and get dressed. He ordered coffee, orange juice, and sweet rolls from room service. The continental breakfast was at the door by the time Susan was dressed.

"The breakfast's for you, to wake you up," he said. "Go ahead and eat while I tell you what to do."

"Want some?" she said, biting into a prune Danish.

"If I'd wanted something I would've ordered it."

Freddy told Susan to drive back to the apartment and to pack up his purchases from the day before and to bring them to the hotel. He told her where he had hidden the coin collection in the leather case, and to bring that, too. Also, while she was home, she could pack a few things she might need herself for a few days' stay at the hotel. "Don't think about it too much. If you forget something, we can always buy it here at Omni. The important thing is to pack my stuff and get the money, then come back here without running into Pablo. He won't be up this early in the morning. On your way back, make sure you aren't followed. If you pick up a tail, lose him before you drive back to the hotel."

"Is somebody after us, Junior?"

"Not us, but me, yes. I'm not a likable person, so someone is usually after me. And because you're with me now, that means somebody'll probably be after you, too."

"I don't understand."

"That isn't important. When there's something important you really need to understand, I'll explain it to you. Right now, when you finish your coffee, I want you to get moving. Here's the extra room key. Change clothes when you get home, too. Wear a skirt and blouse and some saddle shoes."

"What saddle shoes? I don't have any shoes with saddles. I can wear my running shoes."

"Okay. We'll get you some saddle shoes later, so you'll look like a college girl. But that'll be after I deal with Pablo."

"Do I have to see Pablo again? I'm afraid of him."

"Did Pablo fuck you when you first went to work for him?"

"No. I just sucked him off, is all. He wanted to see if I knew how to do it, and then he gave me some pointers, afterward. Pablo knows a lot."

"No, you don't have to see Pablo again. Just beat it now, come back here, and if I'm not here, watch the TV until I get back. If you get hungry, call room service."

After Susan left, Freddy drank what was left of the orange juice. His mouth was still dry. He found it exhausting to talk to Susan, and he was never certain whether she understood everything he told her. Apparently she did, because so far she had done everything right, and she had also picked up on his lies when he had talked to the cop in the Brazilian steak house. But she also had the bad habit of telling the truth when a lie would have done her more good. She shouldn't have told the detective that she was hooking at the hotel. The way she looked, no one would have ever guessed what she did for a living. Later on, when he had more time, he would talk to her about what to say and what not to say; otherwise, she would get herself—and him—into some bad situations.

Freddy called the desk, and found out that the barber shop didn't open until eight-thirty. He took a shower and glumly watched the "Today" show on television until eight A.M. Restless, he got dressed again, and took the elevator to the lobby, sharing the cage with a Latin family with four small children and an old lady with a hairy mole on her chin. The elevator reeked of musk and garlic, and because the rotten kids, on getting in, had pushed all the buttons, the elevator stopped at every floor on the way down.

The barber shop was open. Freddy got a shave. After the shave, the barber combed Freddy's hair and said:

"You have lovely hair, but you really should let it grow. It's much too short for today's stylings."

"Your hair's too long," Freddy said. "You look like a fruit, and if I couldn't tell by your hair, that Swiss army earring you're wearing still gives you away."

Freddy climbed into the first cab in line, and told the old woman who was driving to take him to the International Hotel.

"That's the one on Brickell, isn't it?"

"Are there two International Hotels?"

"Not that I know of—"

"Then it must be the one on Brickell, right?"

"That's what I meant."

People were going to work, and the traffic was heavy. The cab's meter ticked away with the speed of light. When she pulled up at the entrance, Freddy said:

123

"I'm not going to be long. If you want to wait, you can take me over to Miami Beach."

"That beats going to the airport. But you can pay me now, and I'll turn off the meter."

"Don't you trust me?"

"As much as you trust me."

"Keep the meter running." Freddy counted out four twenties. "If it gets up to this much and I'm not back, you can leave without me."

"Yes, sir."

Freddy made a casual tour of the enormous lobby. There were three restaurants and a coffeeshop, three bars, and a dozen specialty shops selling resort clothes and gifts. There was a small conference room next to the Zanzi Bar, with a black-lettered sign outside the door:

BEET SUGAR INSTITUTE
SEMINAR AT 11 A.M.
CASH BAR IN ZANZI BAR AT 10

The Zanzi Bar wasn't open yet, and no one was in the small conference room, although there was a lectern, a movie screen, and thirty or more folding chairs set up for the seminar. Freddy went to a house phone, asked for the bell captain, and waited for him to get on the line.

"Tell Pablo Lhosa," he said to the captain, "to come to the small conference room next to the Zanzi Bar."

"Is anything wrong, sir?"

"Of course not. I'm running the seminar for the beet sugar people, and if anything was wrong I'd call the manager—not Pablo."

"Right away, sir."

The 240-pound Pablo arrived in three minutes, huffing slightly, the two bottom buttons of his monkey jacket unbuttoned because of his belly. Freddy closed the door to the conference room and hit Pablo in the stomach. Pablo gasped and staggered slightly, but he didn't fall. A knife appeared in his right hand. Freddy showed Pablo his badge.

"Put the knife away, Pablo."

Pablo closed the knife and returned it to his pocket.

"My name isn't Gotlieb, Pablo. My name's Sergeant Moseley, Miami Police Department. And that little girl you sent to my room, Susan Waggoner, is only fourteen years old. Your fat ass is in trouble."

"Her brother told me—"

"Her brother's dead, and he lied to you. He was killed at the airport, and it was on the news. You're one of the suspects. Did you have Martin Waggoner hit, Pablo?"

"Hell, no! I didn't—I don't know nothing about it!"

"I've got a signed deposition from Susan that you're her pimp, so your greasy ass is on fire."

"Susie's lying to you, sergeant. She's nineteen, not fourteen. I checked on that. Sergeant Wilson knows I run a few girls here. There's no problem. Why don't you call Sergeant Wilson? I pay him every week. You guys ought to get together."

"Wilson doesn't know you're hustling kids. Susie told me about the pointers you gave her."

"Honest to God, sergeant!" Pablo raised his right arm. "Her brother showed me her driver's license."

"Her brother's dead, and licenses can be forged. Your Cuban ass has *had* it."

"I'm not a Cuban, I'm a Nicaraguan. I was a major in the National Guard. Sergeant Wilson told me—you know Sergeant Wilson, don't you?"

"Fuck Wilson, and fuck you, Pablo. How much're you paying Wilson?"

"Who said I was paying him anything?"

Freddy took out his blackjack and started toward Pablo. Pablo held up his hands and backed away.

"Don't. Please. I give him five hundred a week."

"All right." Freddy put the blackjack away. "I'll let you off the hook, Pablo. From now on, you give Wilson two-fifty a week, and you can send the other two-fifty to me. Just put it in an envelope and send it to me, Sergeant Hoke Moseley, at the Eldorado Hotel. By messenger—not by mail."

Pablo shook his head. "I'll have to talk to Sergeant Wilson first."

"Don't worry about Wilson. I'm the man with Susie's signed deposition, not Wilson."

"I guess you don't know Sergeant Wilson, then. He won't stand for any split like that."

"In that case, it'll cost you seven-fifty a week instead of five hundred, won't it?"

"Give me a break, for Christ's sake!"

"I have. But I'd rather take you in and book you. There're plenty of girls in Miami over eighteen without putting young kids into the life."

"I didn't know. That holy sonofabitch! I asked Marty first thing because she looked so fucking young, but he swore that—"

"Martin Waggoner's dead, Pablo, and there's no one to back you up. You can start paying today. Tonight, by ten P.M. An envelope to the Eldorado Hotel."

"That's in South Beach?"

"That's right, on the bay side, three blocks from Joe's Stone Crabs. Just give it to the man on the desk tonight, and tell him to put it in the safe for me."

"All right, but I'm going to talk to Wilson, and he'll have something to say to you about this."

"I'm sure he will. Tell him if he wants to talk to me, we can meet in the Internal Affairs Office. Tell him that."

"You didn't have to hit me, either."

"I wanted to get your attention, and I thought you might have a knife. Good-bye, Pablo."

Pablo looked as if he might have something more to say, but he turned and left the conference room. He didn't close the door behind him.

He'll send the $250 tonight, Freddy thought, but after his

126

talk with Wilson, whoever that is, he'll probably discontinue the next payment. But maybe not. Sergeant Wilson would worry about those two magic words *Internal Affairs*. Even straight cops were frightened by the investigators in Internal Affairs. At any rate, a confused Pablo Lhosa wouldn't come looking for Susan. As time passed, old Pablo would try to forget that he had ever known her.

The old lady, smoking an aromatic Tijuana Small, was still waiting for Freddy when he came out of the hotel. The meter was ticking away.

"Turn off the meter now," Freddy said, as he got into the back seat. "It reminds me of the passage of time. I'll give you another hundred bucks, and you can give me a tourist's grand tour of Miami Beach. And then, when you get to Bal Harbour, you can drop me at a real estate office."

"I've got nothing better to do," the old lady said.

When Freddy handed her the money she lifted her Mercury Morris T-shirt, with the number 22 on the back, and stuffed the bills into her brassiere.

16

THE WORK ON Hoke's mouth, as planned by Doctors Rubin and Goldstein, did not pan out as well as they had hoped. Hoke's new teeth were almost fragile compared with his old Dolphin choppers; his jaw wouldn't hold a set of heavier teeth. After the jaw healed, and it healed remarkably fast, the restraints were removed and a pan holding evil-tasting pink plaster was jammed into Hoke's mouth. Impressions were made, and twenty-three days after the assault, Hoke had a full set of slightly yellow upper and lower dentures. Hoke had wanted whiter teeth, but Dr. Rubin told him that whiter teeth would look false, and that the yellow ones were more natural for his age.

Nevertheless, when Hoke forced himself to take a long look at his new visage, the teeth looked phony, and he was alarmed by his overall appearance.

Hoke had lost weight on the liquid diet and was down to 158 pounds. The last time he had weighed 158 pounds he had been a junior in high school. He was only forty-two, but with his sunken cheeks and gray beard he thought he looked closer to sixty. The crinkly sun-wrinkles around his eyes were deeper, and the lines from the corners of his nose to the edge of his lips looked as if they had been etched there with a power tool. His habitually dour expression underwent a startling transformation when he smiled: the yellow teeth gave him a sinister appearance.

But Hoke had no reason to smile.

The departmental insurance had covered 80 percent of his hospitalization and a good portion of his dental and surgical fees, but Hoke still owed the hospital and the two doctors more than $10,000. Except for the one night when he had shared the four-bed ward with the teenager, he had had the ward to himself. As a consequence, the hospital had charged him for a private room, except for that one night. On that night, it was charged as a semiprivate room. Hoke's insurance didn't cover a private room, so the "private" room meant an extra $10 a day on his bill. Hoke protested the charge to no avail. When he left the hospital, the nurses packed his bedpan and enema equipment, telling him that he had paid for them and was entitled to take them along.

Before leaving the hospital with Bill Henderson, who had driven over to pick him up, Hoke had a talk with the priest-counselor who wanted to work out some kind of a reasonable monthly payment plan. The talk had ended with both of them angry because Hoke insisted that he couldn't possibly pay more than $25 a month on the enormous bill.

Henderson drove Hoke straight to the Eldorado so he could get his car. The police radio was missing, and so was the battery.

"The department'll put in a new radio, Hoke," Henderson said, "on the strength of a Lost and Damaged Report, but they sure as hell won't get you a new battery."

"There goes another fifty bucks."

"What the hell? You've got the hundred and eighteen bucks the guy didn't find, or didn't want, on top of your dresser, and two paychecks waiting for you in Captain Brownley's office."

"One of those checks goes to my ex-wife," Hoke reminded him. "But what I can't figure out is that money you found in my room. I'll swear that I had less than twenty bucks when I got home. Otherwise I'd've given part of the hundred to Irish Mike to bring down my tab."

"Maybe the guy felt sorry for you. He took your wallet, so he had to take the money out to leave it on your dresser."

"Guys like that don't feel sorry for anyone. Let's go in and talk to Mr. Bennett. And Bill, I really don't want to go home with you. I appreciate your offer, but I'm too much of a loner to put up with Marie and your kids. I want to be alone for the next couple of weeks."

"I thought you might feel that way, so I talked to Mr. Bennett myself. In fact, I won't go inside with you, because Bennett and me—well—we had some words. I got on his ass about the lousy room he had you in, so finally he agreed to give you a small suite on the second floor. Suite two-oh-seven. The old lady who had it for eleven years died."

"Mrs. Schultz died?"

"I think that was her name. Anyway, she had some nice things, and he's left them there and cleaned up the place. You were missed around here while you were in the hospital. The old people were scared shitless when you were attacked. So I guess your Mr. Bennett finally realized that a free security officer was worth two rooms instead of one."

"I guess you knew all along I wouldn't move in on you and Marie?"

"I had a hunch. The main thing was to give you a Miami address, so be sure to use my address on your correspondence. Anyway, I brought all your stuff with me in the trunk of the car, just in case you wanted to stay here."

"Come on in, Bill. You don't have to be worried about Bennett."

Eddie Cohen, the old man who was both night and day desk clerk when he wasn't doing something else, was happy to see Hoke. Eddie rubbed his stubbled chin and pointed to Hoke's gray beard.

"You look like Dr. Freud, Sergeant Moseley."

They shook hands. "Before or after the prosthesis?"

"Before *and* after. You lost yourself a little weight."

"Twenty-seven pounds." Hoke smiled.

"Your new teeth are beautiful! Simply beautiful!"

"Thanks. You know Sergeant Henderson?"

"Oh, yes. We talked the other day. Mr. Bennett said to say welcome back for him. He's up in Palm Beach for the weekend. D'you know about your new suite?"

"Sergeant Henderson just told me."

Eddie shook his head. "Mrs. Schultz went quietly in her sleep. She watched 'Magnum P.I.' in the lobby, went on up to bed, and Mrs. Feeny found her the next morning."

"She was the expert on 'General Hospital' in the TV Club, wasn't she?"

"Right. And 'Dallas,' too."

"My stuff's out in Sergeant Henderson's car. Some sonofabitch stole my radio and battery while I was—"

"No." Cohen shook his head. "Just your radio. I saw the radio was missing on my morning check outside, so I had Gutierrez take out your battery and put it in Mr. Bennett's office. So you've still got your battery. You see," he turned to Henderson, "When they built the Eldorado back in 'twenty-nine, people used to come down here by rail and ship. So there weren't enough cars around then to build parking garages the way they do now.

"Oh, yes, I've also got some money for you."

Eddie Cohen went into the office and returned with two manila envelopes. The flaps were sealed with Scotch tape.

"I opened these when they was delivered, and there was exactly two hundred and fifty dollars in each envelope. I told Mr. Bennett, of course, and we kept the money locked up in the safe. Maybe I shouldn't've opened them"—Eddie shrugged—"but I thought it might be something important."

"That's okay, Eddie," Hoke said. SGT. MOSLEY was

131

printed in capitals with a black felt-tipped pen on each envelope. "Who brought the envelopes?"

"Some Cuban kid on a mini-bike. Both times. He just said to put the envelopes in the safe for Sergeant Moseley. That's all I know. I didn't have to sign a receipt or nothing."

Hoke counted the money on the desk. The bills were all used tens, fives, and singles.

"What's going on, Hoke?" Henderson asked.

"I haven't got a clue. Let's walk over to Irish Mike's and have a drink."

"That's a lot of dough not to know anything about it—"

"I know. Let's talk about it at Irish Mike's. While we're gone, Eddie can get my stuff out of your car. Okay, Eddie?"

"Sure. Go ahead. Gutierrez is around here someplace. He'll take it up for you."

"You said you felt a little weak before," Henderson said. "Can you walk two blocks in the sun?"

"I need to walk off a little adrenaline."

They found seats at the bar in Irish Mike's. Mike shook hands with Hoke, and frowned. "That beard looks terrible, sergeant."

"The doc said to leave it on for a couple of weeks."

Hoke took one of the Manila envelopes out of his leisure jacket pocket and counted out $100 on the bar. He pushed the money across to Irish Mike. "Take care of my tab, and leave what's over as a credit."

"Your credit's always good here, sergeant. You know that. I'll just check your tab and give you back the change."

"No. Leave it. I want to see what it feels like to have a credit for a change. Early Times. Straight up. Water back."

"Similar," Henderson said.

Mike served their drinks and retreated to the other end of the bar to sell a twenty-five-cent punch on his punchboard to a white-bearded old man.

"D'you think it's a good idea to be paying off old debts with money you don't know where it came from, Hoke? Or do you?"

"Do I, what?"

"Know where the money came from. That's a lot of money. You aren't into something you haven't told me about, are you?"

"I don't know where it came from, and I don't care. Maybe you guys in the division took up a collection for me?"

"That'll be the fucking day. First you find an extra hundred on your dresser you don't know about, and then you get a couple of two-fifty payoffs in anonymous brown envelopes. It must've come from the guy who clobbered you."

"I hope so. But it's no payoff, Bill. Maybe the bastard feels guilty. If so, it's because he assaulted the wrong man. I've gone over every case I could think of in the last ten years. Lying in the hospital, I've had plenty of time to think, and I couldn't think of anyone who'd lay for me like that. There're a couple of guys who might've been happy to kill me, but that's what they would've done. A beating like the one I got wouldn't've been enough."

"Even so, Hoke, if it was me, I'd be damned leery of spending any of that dough till I found out where it came from."

"Fuck where it came from. I need it, and I can use it. I'll be in Monday to pick up my paychecks, but Captain Brownley said to take two weeks' sick leave before coming back to duty. And that's what I'm going to do. How's your new partner Lopez working out?"

"Lopez is a Cuban, for Christ's sake. He saw *The French Connection,* so now he wears his gun in an ankle holster the way Popeye did in the movie."

"No shit?" Hoke bared his yellow teeth in a smile.

"God's truth. Let's have the other half." Henderson signaled to Irish Mike for two more, and took out his wallet.

"Put your money away," Hoke said. "I've got a credit going here."

GUTIERREZ HAD PUT all of Hoke's clothing away neatly by the time Hoke returned to his new suite. It was a small suite, all right, even with the sitting room, and it looked even smaller because the late Mrs. Schultz had crammed a great many purchases from garage sales into the sitting room during her eleven years of residence. There was a comfortable Victorian armchair stuffed with horsehair, where Hoke could sit and watch his little Sony, and there was a handsome rolltop desk with a matching swivel chair, flush against the wall. Hoke put his files and papers into the desk drawers, happy to have a desk in his room. In his tiny room on the eighth floor, he had had to unfold a bridge table that he kept under the bed, when he wanted to eat or to do some paperwork at home. The brass bed in the bedroom was full-size, too, which meant that he could bring a woman to his room and not be embarrassed.

Hoke took out his dentures, which irritated his gums, and put them to soak in a plastic glass with some Polident. Dr. Rubin had said it would take a little time to get used to them and to note the rough spots, if any, and they could be adjusted on Hoke's next visit to the office. Hoke examined his face in the mirror and was appalled. Without his dentures, he looked even worse. His gray beard, almost an inch long, reminded him of Mr. Geezil in the old "Popeye" comic strip. His chances of ever getting a woman into his new brass bed seemed negligible, and he hadn't been laid for five months. With a sigh, Hoke left the bathroom.

There was a single window air conditioner in the bedroom, but very little cold air filtered into the sitting room. If he couldn't wangle another room air conditioner from Mr. Bennett, he would have to buy an overhead fan. On the wall above the desk, there was a large painting of three white horses pulling a fire truck. The horses' nostrils flared, and their eyes rolled wildly. That was one hell of a painting, Hoke decided, and probably worth a lot of money.

He was surprised that Mr. Bennett had left it in the room instead of selling it—

There was a rapping on the door—three sharp peremptory knocks.

Hoke panicked. He pulled open drawers in the desk, ripping a fingernail in the process, forgetting for a frenzied moment or so that his gun had been stolen. What could he use as a weapon? There was a heavy glass paperweight on the desk, with a butterfly preserved in its interior. Hoke snatched it up and stood with his back against the wall beside the door.

"Who is it?" Hoke said.

"Sergeant Wilson," a deep voice rumbled. "Miami Police Department."

"Slide your ID under the door."

"Are you kidding?"

"Try me. The next thing you hear, if you hear anything, will be a bullet through the door!"

"Je-sus Christ!" The deep voice was disgusted.

A moment later, the ID card with Wilson's photograph on it was slipped beneath the door. Hoke picked it up. It showed that Wilson was black, six feet, two inches tall, 230 pounds, and a sergeant in the MPD, Vice Division. He was also ugly. His nose was almost as wide as his lips, and he had a boxer's cauliflower ears.

Hoke took off the chain lock and opened the door. The man reached for his ID card. He held his badge in his other hand. He took the ID card from Hoke's fingers and put it back in his card case; then he put his badge away.

"What's up, sergeant?" Wilson said. "You got a guilty conscience?"

"I just came home from the hospital."

"I know. I checked. You also got something that belongs to me. Let's have it."

"I don't know what you're talking about. I've never seen you before."

"I've seen you. I'm in Vice, and you've been moving into my territory. Let me have the envelopes, please." He held out a huge hand.

Hoke was puzzled. If Hoke had been paid off by mistake, how could anybody take him for Sergeant Wilson? Whoever it was who mixed them up had to be colorblind or badly misinformed.

"The envelopes addressed to me?"

"The ones addressed to you."

Hoke handed over the two brown envelopes. Sergeant Wilson counted the money. "It's a hundred dollars short."

Hoke cleared his throat. "I spent a little."

"Give me your wallet."

"Fuck you."

With the flat of his palm, Wilson pushed Hoke into the swivel chair by the desk and held him there with very little effort. Hoke struggled, realized how weak he was, and slumped back into the chair. Wilson took the wallet out of Hoke's hip pocket, counted out $100, and tossed the wallet on the desk. He put the bills into the brown envelope and then put both envelopes into the breast pocket of his beige silk sports jacket.

"Pablo wants the girl back, too, old timer. Make sure she's back at the International Hotel by ten A.M. tomorrow, and all will be forgotten. Not forgiven, but forgotten. Otherwise . . ." He looked around the room and shook his head. "I guess you're desperate for dough, livin' in a dump like this, but you must've been crazy to fuck with me."

Wilson checked the bedroom and then took a quick look into the bathroom. He noticed Hoke's false teeth in the plastic glass. He dumped the water into the sink, opened the window in the sitting room, pushed out the screen, and tossed the teeth out the window.

Hoke almost asked, what girl? But he knew that the girl was Susan Waggoner. And he knew now who had put him in the hospital. He didn't know why, and he didn't know why he'd been sent money, but he intended to find out.

136

Wilson closed the door softly behind him as he left the room.

It took Hoke twenty minutes to find his teeth, but they had landed in a cluster of screw-leaved crotons and weren't damaged. He put them into a fresh glass of water with another helping of Polident and wondered what in the hell he was going to do next.

17

AFTER THE CAB tour of Collins Avenue in Miami Beach, Mrs. Freeman made a brief stop so that Freddy could take a closer look at Lincoln Road, the once famous and now deteriorated shopping mall. Freddy suggested a late breakfast.

"You ever eat at Manny's?" Mrs. Freeman said. "You can get a crabmeat omelet, and they give you a basket of hot rolls with butter and honey. And it's the only place left on the Beach with free coffee refills."

"Sounds good," Freddy nodded. "I used to eat crabmeat omelets a long time ago on Fisherman's Wharf, when I lived in San Francisco."

Manny's was tucked away between a four-story kosher spa and a boarded-up two-story warehouse. Mrs. Freeman parked her cab in the weedy warehouse lot and they went into Manny's. The fish odor inside was strong. Mrs. Freeman ordered the crabmeat omelet, but Freddy shook his head.

"I've changed my mind. Give me a Denver omelet."

"What's that?" the Pakistani waiter asked.

"It's eggs scrambled up with chopped ham, green peppers, and onions."

"What he wants," Mrs. Freeman said, "is a western omelet."

"That we got," the waiter said, and went off to the kitchen.

"In California, we call it a Denver omelet."

"So you're from California?"

"What makes you say that?"

"You just said, 'In California—'"

"Just because I said that I'd been *in* California doesn't have to mean that I'm *from* California. People are too quick to imply bad things about people before they've thought them out."

"So you live in Miami, then?" Mrs. Freeman shook her gray curls. Her gray dentures had a translucent quality. Her pale blue eyes were clear.

"Yeah. What I'm looking for is a nice little house, but what I've seen of Miami Beach so far doesn't appeal to me. What's up a little farther north?"

"Well, after we pass Bal Harbour, WASP territory, we start to hit Motel Row. The Thunderbird, The Aztec, theme places like that. They cater mostly to Canadian and British blue-collar vacationers in the summer, and American families down here on the cheap during the season. Mostly families from New York, Jersey, and Pennsylvania. But if you're looking for a little house to rent, we can go on past the row and over to Dania. There're some nice little houses there, and it's a quiet town, too, except for the jai alai fronton."

"We'll take a look."

"What they do in Dania, they sell antiques. There're dozens of little antique shops along US 1. Fakes mostly, but the furniture's a lot better made nowadays than the real thing used to be."

"I like new furniture."

"Well, that's what you buy in Dania. New antiques."

Freddy liked the looks of Dania. The small stucco homes reminded him of southwest Los Angeles, down around

Slauson and Figueroa. The main street was also US 1, which would give him a straight shot into Miami, where US 1 became Biscayne Boulevard. He told Mrs. Freeman to cruise slowly up and down the tree-shaded streets so he could look for For Rent and For Sale signs. There were several, but Freddy told her to stop at a small white house surrounded by a white picket fence. There were two towering mango trees in the front yard, and the owner had planted a border of geraniums alongside the house on both sides of the front door. There was an attached garage as well.

Freddy knocked on the door and negotiated with the owner. She was a widow whose husband had died recently, and she wanted to sell the house and move back to Cincinnati to live with her daughter and son-in-law. Until she sold the house, she wouldn't have enough money to leave.

"I don't know whether I want to buy or not," Freddy said, "but I'll tell you what I'll do. I'll rent it for a couple of months, and then if I like it you can give me an option to buy it. If I don't buy, you'll still have two months' rent money to spend, and you can leave for Cincinnati right away. How much are you willing to rent it for?"

"I don't really know," the widow said. "Would two hundred and fifty be too much?"

"That's not nearly enough. I'll give you five hundred a month, in advance, and you can leave the furniture, pack up, and go on up to Cincinnati tonight."

"I don't know that I can get ready that soon—"

Freddy counted out $1,000 on the fake cobbler's bench.

"But I guess I can make it all right," she said quickly, scooping up the money. Freddy got a receipt, and after two phone calls the widow said she could be out of the house by ten that night, and that she would leave the keys next door when she left. Freddy returned to the cab and told Mrs. Freeman he had rented the little house.

"Furnished or unfurnished?"

"Furnished."

"How many bedrooms?"

"One, I think, but I didn't look. There's a big screened porch out back, too."

"I'm not trying to pry into your business, mister, it's just that you're so innocent-like. How much is she charging you?"

"What's it to you? You're a nosy old bat, Mrs. Freeman. Did anybody ever tell you that?"

"Lots of times. You should've let me negotiate for you. They call this town Dania because it was settled by Danes, and it takes a Jew to outsmart a Dane. That's all I'm saying."

"I never question prices. Money's too easy to get in Miami. That's why the prices are so high down here."

"In that case," she said, shaking her curls, "you can give me a ten-dollar tip when I drop you off at the Omni."

When they reached the Omni, Freddy gave the old lady a $10 tip. "You're not as sharp as you think you are, Mrs. Freeman. I was going to give you a twenty."

Her high, cackling laughter followed him into the lobby.

SUSAN, WEARING WHITE cut-offs and a KISS T-shirt, was eating a tuna salad sandwich and drinking a Tab when Freddy unlocked the door and came into the room. The bed had been made, the curtains were drawn back, and the room was delightfully cool.

"Why aren't you watching TV?" Freddy said.

"I was. I did the exercises with Richard Simmons, switched over to cable, and then did aerobics for five minutes. And that was enough TV for me. I sent your pants with the little tennis rackets and your blue guayabera to the cleaners. They'll be back by three, the boy said."

"Good. I like that. I've been out getting oriented and thinking about what to do, so I rented us a little house up in Dania."

"By the fronton?"

141

"No, but it's only about eight blocks away. Maybe we can go some night. I've never seen any jai alai. They don't have it in California. Not that I know of, anyway."

"The first game you see is exciting. But after the first game it's almost as boring as watching greyhounds."

"We'll go anyway. But I don't want to talk about that right now. Let me have the rest of that Tab. It's hotter than a sonofabitch outside. What I wanted to ask you was this—" Freddy finished the Tab. "You said your girl friends up in Okeechobee got married, right?"

"Most did, those who didn't leave for someplace else, or just stay home and mope around. There isn't much choice up in Okeechobee."

"What do they do then, after they're married, I mean?"

"Take care of the house, shop, fix dinner. Sue Ellen, who was in the eleventh grade with me, has three babies already."

"Is that what you want? Babies?"

"Not anymore. Once I did, but not since the abortion. I'm on the pill, and I use foam besides—unless the john says he wants to go down on me. But now that we're married, I guess I can go off the pill and quit using the foam, too."

"No, stay on the pill. I don't want any babies either, but if you did, I thought I might try it that way some time. Right now, I like the way we're doing it."

Susan blushed happily. "Would you like the other half of this tuna sandwich?"

"No. I had a western omelet for a late breakfast. What else do the married girls do up in Okeechobee?"

"Not a lot, the girls I ran around with. They don't work because there isn't much work there to speak of, and their husbands wouldn't want them to, anyway. It makes a guy look bad if his wife has to work, unless they're in business together or something and she has to help him out, sort of. They visit their mothers, shop at the K-Mart, or go roller-skating at the rink sometimes over at Clewiston. On weekends there're barbecues and fish fries. I guess the married girls my age do the same things they did in high school, except they just go with one guy, and that's usually the same guy they were fucking all the way through high school anyway. The best thing, though, they get away from home and their parents. They can stay up late and sleep late, too. If it hadn't been for Marty, I probably would've been married now."

"Okay, so let's say we're married, which we are, though it's a platonic marriage. Is that what you'd like to do? Keep a house, fix regular meals, go shopping? I know you're a good cook. I liked those stuffed pork chops a lot."

Susan smiled and looked at her wriggling toes. "I did all the cooking at home. You just wait till you taste my chuck roast, with sherry in the gravy! I make it in the Crockpot with little pearl onions, new potatoes, and chopped celery and parsley. I use just a tiny pinch of curry powder—that's the secret to Crockpot chuck roast."

"It sounds okay."

"It is good, too, let me tell you."

"I've never been married before." Freddy took off his jacket and kicked off his Ballys. "I lived with a woman for about two months once. She never cooked anything or kept house or did much of anything a wife's supposed to do. But when I came home you see, she was someone to be there. I came back one night and found that she'd left, taking the five hundred bucks I had stashed under the carpet with her. I was going to look for her, and then I realized that I was damned lucky to get rid of her so easily. She was a junkie, so I didn't try to find her.

"I had a Filipino boy living with me once, too, in Oakland. But he was a jealous little bastard, and he questioned me all the time. I don't like to be questioned, you know."

"I know."

"What I'm getting at, Susie, or what I want, is a regular life. I want to go to work in the morning, or maybe at night,

143

and come home to a clean house, a decent dinner, and a loving wife like you. I don't want any babies. The world's too mean to bring another kid into it, and I'm not that irresponsible. The niggers and the Catholics don't care, but somebody's got to—d'you know what I mean? Do you think you can handle it?''

Susan began to cry and nod her head. "Yes, oh, yes, that's what I always wanted, too, Junior. And I'll be a good wife to you, too. You just wait and see!''

"All right, then. I'm going to take a shower. You can stop crying and pack everything, and then we can get moving. If you think you're happy now, wait'll you see the little house I've got for you in Dania.''

Susan wiped her eyes. "But what about your shirt and pants I sent to the cleaners?''

"The bellboy'll hang 'em in the closet. I'm not giving up this nice room. It'll be an office for me, because most of my work'll be in the Omni shopping mall.''

But it wasn't that simple. The widow in Dania, as it turned out, couldn't leave for two more days. They spent those two days shopping for things they needed for the house, including a new microwave oven for Susan. Then, when they did get into the house, the water and electricity had been turned off, and it took Susan an entire morning to find the water company and Florida Power to put down deposits. There was also the gas company to contact, and they had to have a man come out to fill the propane tank outside the kitchen window.

Freddy also sent Susan to the bank to exchange the ten thousand pesos he had lifted from the Mexican pickpocket, but she brought the money back.

"The man at the bank told me they weren't changing pesos anymore," Susan said. "He said my best bet would be to go out to the airport and find someone who was going to Mexico and to made a deal with him. Should I?''

"I think not. The airport's too dangerous to be bothering

the tourists out there. Remember what happened to your brother? Just put the pesos back in the Ritz cracker box with the rest of the money."

When they got into the house, Freddy streamlined the house by moving everything he didn't like into the garage. Susan wanted a telephone, but Freddy didn't.

"If we had one," he said, "who would we call?"

"The repairman for the washer. The washer works okay, but there's a leak in it or something because there's always a big pool of water after every load. And you might get in trouble sometime and want to call me from jail or something."

"Don't put a damned jinx on me."

"I'm not, but a house isn't like an apartment where you can always call the manager to fix something. We've got a septic tank out front. Did you see the bright green grass in the big square patch under the mango tree outside the living room? That's where it is, and I'll bet you those roots are breaking through the tiles. If you treat 'em right, septic tanks work like magic, but if you don't, they'll back shit up through the john and fill the whole house."

"Get a phone, then. But put it in your name, not mine."

Susan wanted the car; so did Freddy. They compromised and Susan drove Freddy to the Omni every morning at nine. She picked him up at four P.M. and brought him back to Dania.

In the mornings, Freddy would go directly to his hotel room and change into slacks, running shoes, and a sports shirt with long square tails. The tails covered the holstered pistol he wore at his back, and the handcuffs on his belt were also hidden. He carried the sap in his right hip pocket, and his badge and ID in his right front pocket.

He got to know each shopping level well, and he had escape routes mentally mapped out for quick getaways from each floor. He was soon able to tell vacationing South Americans from permanent Miami Latin residents. He could spot the South American men by their dark suits; and

145

the women did not, for the most part, have that little shelf above their buttocks that Cuban and Puerto Rican women had. If he was unsure, he could listen to them talk: the South Americans spoke Spanish softer and slower than the Cubans.

He came to realize how lucky he had been on that first day when he had mugged the Mexico City pickpocket.

There were a good many security people working the mall, some in uniform, and others in plain clothes. He could almost set his watch by the security officer in Penney's. The man wore a billed fisherman's cap, a flowered sports shirt, and jeans. He spent an average of fifteen minutes on each floor and took fifteen-minute breaks at 10:30 A.M. and 3:30 P.M. in the employees' lounge. Every day at lunchtime he ordered the special, whatever it happened to be, in the deli on Level Three.

There were others, Freddy was sure, who were not that regular and much harder to spot. If they didn't have uniforms, they could be damned near anybody. But Freddy felt protected with Sergeant Moseley's buzzer in his pocket. The lost badge was undoubtedly on the computer of the Miami Police Department, and any Miami cop might question it, but the MPD didn't pass on that kind of information to the private agencies that firms like Omni International and the department stores hired. So, if he got into any trouble, all he had to do was flash the buzzer, and he could get out of almost any situation.

During his first three days of work at the Omni, the only thing Freddy managed to steal was a package he took out of an unlocked station wagon on Rose Two. Later, when he opened the package in his hotel room, he found two pairs of kid's jeans, size eight, husky. He gave the jeans to one of the Jamaican maids.

His fourth day of work was also frustrating. That night after dinner he took the TransAm and drove around the city, then broke into an appliance store on Twenty-seventh Avenue. The alarm went off the moment he heaved a

146

concrete block through the wire-mesh window of the back door. He reached in and opened the door, and grabbed an RCA color TV set and two electric digital clocks. Forty minutes later, when he cruised slowly by the store, driving in the opposite direction, the alarm bell was still ringing and the cops had still not investigated.

Susan hooked up the TV set to the aerial that was already on the house, and the set worked fine, except for a snowy Channel 2, but neither of the digital clocks kept accurate time.

The next day was better. Freddy caught two pot peddlers in the Jordan Marsh restroom on the second floor. They were arguing fiercely about money when he came in and didn't even look in his direction until he had them covered with his .38.

"Freeze. Police," Freddy said.

They froze. He took their wallets and six ounces of marijuana in a plastic Baggie. He handcuffed both of them, left wrist and right wrist, around the pipe in the first toilet stall, and left the restroom. He would have left the keys to the handcuffs just out of their reach, but he didn't have them. They could explain their situation to whoever it was that rescued them, he supposed, but at least he had plenty of time to get back to his room in the Omni Hotel.

There were $300 in cash, four $50 unsigned traveler's checks, and a gold St. Christopher's medal in the wallets. There were no credit cards, and only one driver's license —a license for Angel Salome. The wallets weren't worth keeping, and neither was the driver's license, but the small medal was a nice gift for Susan. The unsigned traveler's checks were good to have, and it was the first time he had ever seen completely blank checks like that, which a man could sign with any name he wanted.

Susan settled in very quickly to a domestic routine. She cooked ample breakfasts for Freddy, surprising him with Belgian walnut waffles, shirred eggs, and French toast made with sourdough bread. Then, after she dropped him off at the Omni, she shopped at the supermarkets, cleaned house, and planned her dinners. One day she was able to buy Okeechobee catfish, which she fried, together with hush puppies, and she served steak fries and collard greens on the side. Freddy didn't like the catfish because of the bones, but he enjoyed the other meals she prepared. She always topped off the dinners with tart desserts, too, like Granny Smith apple pie, bubbly with butter, brown sugar, and cinnamon. One night she baked a turkey breast and served it with all the trimmings, including a mince pie that she baked from scratch.

She washed and ironed the clothes and sheets, and started a small vegetable garden in the back yard, planting cucumbers, radishes, and a single row of tomato plants along the back fence. She made friends with Mrs. Edna Damrosch, the widow next door, who worked as a saleslady in a Dania antique store on Wednesdays and Saturdays.

On the days Mrs. Damrosch didn't work and when Freddy wasn't home, they visited each other's houses to watch soap operas and to discuss the lives of the characters.

One night Susan cooked fried chicken. She planned to serve cheese grits, Stove-Top dressing, canned peas, and milk gravy with the chicken but discovered she was out of milk. She grabbed her purse and asked Freddy for the car keys. Freddy was watching the news on television and, as usual when he was home, was wearing only jeans. There was a window air conditioner in the bedroom, but none in the living room where the TV had been set up, and the room was always warm and stuffy.

"Where do you want to go?"

"I just want to run down to the Seven-Eleven for some milk."

"Fix iced tea instead."

"I need milk for the gravy."

"I'll go. You'd better stay here and watch what you're cooking."

Freddy, without putting on a shirt or his shoes, picked up

his wallet and the keys from the cobbler's bench and drove the six blocks to the nearest 7-Eleven. He went to the dairy case, deliberated for a moment on whether to buy a quart or a half-gallon of milk, and then slid back the glass door. A short stickup man entered the store, held a gun on the manager, and told him in Spanish to give him the money in the register. The stickup man, in his early twenties, was very nervous, and the gun danced in his shaking hand.

The frightened manager, without a word, gave the gunman the $36 in the till. The stickup man put the bills in his pocket and backed toward the glass double doors. He then stuck the pistol in his waistband and took four cartons of cigarettes from a counter display. He noticed Freddy for the first time. Startled, he dropped the cigarettes and reached for his pistol again. Freddy, reacting impulsively, picked up a can of Campbell's pork and beans and threw it at the gunman, who turned sideways, just in time. The can hit the window, narrowly missing the man's left shoulder.

The glass shattered and a triangular sliver of glass gashed the man's throat. It was a shallow cut, but it began to bleed. The man dropped his gun, clutched his neck, and rushed through the double doors. Freddy went after him, but as the man got into the passenger seat of a heavy Chevrolet Impala, the driver drove forward and up over the curb, heading for the doors. By the time Freddy skirted the stacked bread shelves and reached the doorway, so had the car bumper. Both doors crashed down on Freddy as the driver rammed them. The car then backed away and careened into the street. The falling doors slammed Freddy onto the floor and pinned him. The manager lifted off the doors, and Freddy got shakily to his feet. As the manager hurried to the phone, Freddy got into his car and drove home—without the milk.

When he got home, Freddy gave Susan the car keys and wrote out a list of supplies for her to get at Eckerd's drugstore. He turned off the gas under the food in the kitchen before going into the bathroom to check his injuries.

His left wrist was sprained badly, but he didn't think it was broken. There might be a hairline fracture, but he didn't think it was any worse than that. There were a dozen cuts on his face, however, and more on his chest where his chest had been scraped by shards of glass. The worst thing was his right eyebrow. The eyebrow, skin and all, was one big flap hanging down over his eye. He would have to sew it back on and hope that it would grow together again. The other cuts in his face were not only deep, they were penetrating punctures, but they wouldn't require stitches. The cuts on his chest were ridged scrapes, but not as deep as the punctures on his face, so he figured they would scab over within a few days.

When Susan got back, he asked her to thread the smallest needle in the packet with black thread. He sewed the eyebrow flap on to his forehead with small stitches. Susan watched the first stitch and then vomited into the toilet bowl.

"That doesn't help me much, you know," he said. "Go into the bedroom and lie down."

The flap, after he had put as many stitches into it as he thought it would hold, was more than a little crooked, and the eyebrow slanted up at a curious angle, but that was about the best he could do. He was in considerable pain, but he felt lucky that he hadn't lost the eye. By midnight, he knew that the entire eye area would be black and blue. His face was swelling already. He dabbed at his face cuts with balls of cotton soaked in peroxide, and when all of the cuts had stopped trickling blood, he plastered them with Band-Aids. Susan had bought the kind that were blue and red and dotted with white stars, and he ended up with fourteen patriotic Band-Aids on his face and neck. He washed his chest with a washrag, and then with peroxide, but decided not to bandage the scrapes.

His sprained wrist was now twice its normal size. He had Susan splint it with tongue depressors and bind it as tightly as she could with strips of adhesive tape. He could move his fingers, but it hurt. He sent her back to Eckerd's to get a canister of plaster of Paris and cut pieces of gauze into eight-inch strips while she was gone. When she returned, they mixed the plaster with water, soaked the strips of gauze, and he had her wrap them in overlapping strips around his wrist. The cast, when she finished, was thick and heavy, but when it dried it would immobilize his arm just in case there was a hairline fracture. Freddy took three Bufferin, then ate some fried chicken, although he had no appetite for it.

"Are you going to tell me about it, Junior?"

"About how dumb I was, d'you mean? Sure, I'll tell you about it. I forgot for a minute that Miami, like any other city, is a dangerous place. I didn't take my gun to the store, not even my sap. Not only that, I broke my own rule, and I tried to help someone else instead of looking after my own ass. This straight life we've been leading has given me a misplaced sense of security, that's all. For a moment there, I must've thought that I was some kind of solid citizen. That's all."

"But what *happened* to you?"

"Two guys in a blue Impala ran over me."

Susan nodded but looked thoughtful. "I thought it must've been something like that."

18

MARIE HENDERSON WAS active in a Miami NOW chapter and had a subscription to *Ms.* magazine. When Bill Henderson had first told Hoke that his wife was subscribing to *Ms.*, Hoke didn't believe him, so Henderson brought one of her copies down to the office and showed him the printed address label. It was made out to Ms. Marie Henderson.

"That's incredible," Hoke had said, shaking his head morosely at the irrefutable evidence.

"Isn't it?" Henderson agreed. "Now you've got some kind of idea of what I have to put up with . . ."

Hoke parked at the curb in front of Henderson's ranch-style house. He didn't see Henderson's car in the carport. He walked reluctantly up the brick walk to knock on the door anyway. Perhaps, he thought, Bill wouldn't be gone very long.

Marie Henderson, a tall bony woman of thirty-eight with brown, frizzy hair, seemed happy enough to see Hoke. She invited him in, pointed toward Henderson's comfortable recliner, and asked him if he would like a drink.

"Sure," Hoke nodded. "Early Times, if you've got it."

"We've got it." She brought a bottle of Early Times and two shot glasses from the bar and put them on the coffee table in front of him. She went into the kitchen and returned with a pitcher of ice and water.

"That's the way Bill drinks it—straight with water back, so I suppose you do, too."

"Yeah. It gives you a little lift this way."

"I'm sure it does." Marie smiled. "You don't look too bad, Hoke. Bill said you looked like death warmed over. The beard could do with some trimming."

"The doctor said to leave it on for a while."

"He didn't tell you not to trim it, did he? You know who you remind me of with that beard? Ray Milland. Did you see that picture when he was sick and in a wheelchair? His daughter was a librarian, and he had her wait on him hand and foot. The way it turned out, he didn't need the wheelchair at all. He was faking it to make a slave out of his daughter. Finally, the girl pushed him over a cliff and got all the money he was hoarding in a cigar box under his bed, or something. Did you see it?"

"No, I didn't see it."

"Well, you didn't miss much. It was on the cable a couple of months ago. If it comes back, I'll call you."

"I don't have cable. I saw Ray Milland in *Love Story*, when he played the father, but I don't remember exactly how he looked."

"He looked good then. That was several years ago. But you look a lot like him now, something about your smile, I think."

"Thanks. When is Bill coming back?"

"He's out bowling. He's not on a regular team, but when Green Lakes Landscaping is short a man, they come by and get Henderson. He's only got a one-thirty average, so they don't come by for him often."

"He did tell me that he was doing some bowling for the exercise."

"Bowling for two hours once or twice a month isn't too much exercise, is it?"

153

"I guess not. When'll he be home? Maybe I'd better come back later?"

"Stick around. He'll be home soon. Pour yourself another drink."

"How're the kids, Marie?"

"Out, I'm happy to say."

Hoke had two more drinks before Henderson came home, but there was no more conversation because Hoke and Marie had run out of things to talk about.

When Henderson came in, carrying his bowling ball and bowling shoes in a blue nylon bag, Marie got up from her chair and went into the kitchen. Hoke rose quickly. He was a trifle dizzy and feeling the effects of three drinks.

"Did Captain Brownley get a hold of you?" Bill asked as he got a shot glass from the bar.

"No. I've been here for almost an hour."

Bill poured a drink, and tossed it down. "I tried to get you before I left. I let the phone ring about fifteen times, and no one answered. What kind of a hotel is that, anyway?"

"Sometimes Eddie's doing something else, and he isn't on the switchboard. I told Mr. Bennett he needs someone on the desk all the time, but he says the old people don't get that many calls. The Eldorado's probably got the smallest staff of any hotel on the Beach. So what's up, Bill?"

"You're here, so that's why I thought Brownley had called you. Sit down a minute. I'll be right back." Bill left the room and returned a few moments later with a large brown envelope, which he handed to Hoke. Hoke opened the envelope and took out a pair of handcuffs.

"Are those yours?" Bill asked. "There's an *M* in red fingernail polish on the right cuff—"

"Yeah." Hoke nodded. "They're mine all right. Remember Bambi, the woman in the Grove I was sleeping with about two years back? We were playing a little game one night and—well, anyway, I used her nail polish to mark one cuff. Where'd you get them?"

"Robbery. They've had 'em for a few days. Two guys were cuffed together in the men's john in Jordan Marsh, in the Omni store. They claimed they were cuffed up by some crazy cop who took their money. The Robbery people just figured these two guys were into something kinky and let them go. Then, a couple of days later, one of the detectives in Robbery happened to notice the initial, and remembered the red-liner memo on your lost buzzer and pistol. He sent the cuffs over to Captain Brownley through interoffice mail. So that's that."

"No, Bill, it's much worse than that."

Hoke filled Henderson in on Sergeant Wilson's visit, and told him about the order to get the girl, Susan, back to the International Hotel in the morning. Still sensitive about his fragile, ill-fitting teeth, he omitted the part about Wilson throwing them out of the window.

"This guy's trying to get you into trouble, Hoke. It may be the girl's boyfriend, and maybe not. Why, though, is something else. One guy I really know is Wilson. He was in Vice when I was still in Vice, and he's a vicious sonofabitch. Mean, but I always thought he was straight. I haven't seen him in a couple of years, however, and a lot can happen to a man in two years."

Hoke scratched his bearded jaw. "In two seconds a lot can happen to a man."

"What're you going to do about Wilson?"

"I don't know. I could go to Brownley with it, but how do I explain the five hundred bucks?"

"You just tell it like it happened, and you're covered. I was there, and I can back up your story. It links up with the way this guy—what's his name?"

"Mendez. Only that isn't his name."

"Anyway, it links in with the way he used your cuffs to rob two bastards and leave 'em in the john. If you want me to, we can leave Brownley out of it, and I'll talk to Wilson."

"If you could get across to him that he's after the wrong guy—"

"I will. But it won't be all that easy because you were spending his money."

"I didn't know it was Wilson's. Besides, he got his five hundred back. I can't get the girl back and wouldn't if I could."

"I'll talk to him. I know how to deal with a prick like that."

"I appreciate that, Bill."

"D'you have a gun?"

"I get my new gun and shield back Monday, when I see Captain Brownley."

"I'll get you one. I've got a chrome Colt thirty-two automatic you can have. I used to carry it in Liberty City in case I needed a throw-down piece. It's not much good, but the magazine holds seven rounds."

"I can give it back to you on Monday. It really feels funny as hell driving and walking around Miami without a weapon."

"I can imagine."

Henderson got the .32 out of the desk in the dining room and gave it to Hoke. Hoke removed the magazine, checked the chamber, and then slipped the magazine in again and loaded the pistol with a round in the chamber. He flipped up the safety with his thumb and put the weapon into his hip pocket.

"In case you're interested, Hoke, I gave Martin Waggoner's effects to his father when he took the body back to Okeechobee. I used my key to your desk."

"That's okay, but what about the Krishnas?"

"They didn't have any claims." Henderson smiled. "I called the head honcho out there when I didn't hear from them, and I got the impression that Martin Waggoner was a novice, not a full member, and was about to be thrown out anyway."

"Did he tell you that?"

"Not in so many words, but that's the impression the honcho gave me. He wasn't even interested in the funeral arrangements, even though I told him what Mr. Waggoner had in mind."

"Martin was probably ripping them off. That's some family, isn't it? Incest, prostitution, fanaticism, software. . . . I'd better go home, Bill. This is really only my first day to be traipsing around, and I'm bushed as hell."

"Want me to drive you home?"

"Hell, no. I just mean that I'm tired. Otherwise I'm okay."

"Be careful, Hoke. This guy, this Mendez, or whatever his name is, seems like a crazy bastard to me. And when he finds out that you're up and around, he might come after you again."

"I'll watch myself all right, don't worry."

Hoke was almost certain that the man from California was after him, but he couldn't figure out why. He didn't feel safe until he got home and had locked the door and bolted it behind him.

ON SUNDAY, HOKE stayed in bed almost all day. He braved the heat at noon and walked to Gold's Deli for the Sunday chicken-in-the-pot special, but he napped again during the afternoon. At six, he made his regular rounds of the hotel and discovered that Mr. Bennett had, during his absence in the hospital, put chains and a padlock around the quick-release handles to the back fire door exit. Hoke got the keys from the office, unlocked the chains, and put them into the storage room behind the unused kitchen. Later, when he made out his report and put it on Mr. Bennett's desk, he reminded the manager that the fire marshal could close the hotel down for a serious violation like that.

For dinner, Hoke heated a can of Chunky Turkey Soup on the hot plate in his room, and then watched "Archie Bunker's Place" on television. After the show, he called Bill Henderson.

"Everything's okay, Hoke," Henderson said. "I talked to Wilson last night, explained things to him, and he'll be on the lookout for Mendez himself."

"I don't think that's his real name."

"All right, all right! What do we call him then?"

"I'm sorry. Mendez, I guess."

"Anyway, Wilson wants to find him as much as we do now. Apparently the guy scared the hell out of Pablo, and Wilson told me that Pablo's talking about going back to Nicaragua. I also reassured Wilson that neither one of us is going to say anything to Internal Affairs. We've got enough to do in Homicide without worrying about what's going on in Vice. He also told me to tell you he's sorry about your teeth."

"I'm sorry about them, too. I have to pour hot sauce on everything now in order to get any taste."

"How you feeling otherwise?"

"Okay. I'll probably see you in the morning when I come in to get my gun and badge from Brownley."

"I don't think so. I'll be out with Lopez. We're doing that investigation about the woman who sat on her kid, and I'm letting him handle it. But I'm watching him."

"What case is that?"

"It was in the papers. This woman was punishing her kid, a six-year-old, and she sat on him. She weighs about two-forty, and she crushed in his chest. The kid died, and now she's up for manslaughter. It'll probably be reduced to child abuse, but we've got to knock on doors all morning to see what the neighbors've got to say about her and the kid."

"Did she do it on purpose?"

"I think so. But Lopez, being Cuban, doesn't. Cubans, he says, don't punish their kids no matter what they do, so he thinks it was an accident. We'll find out after we've knocked on a few doors. Incidentally, I found out who your new partner's going to be. Ellita Sanchez. D'you know her?"

"The dispatcher? The girl with the big tits?"

"Girl? She's at least thirty, Hoke, and she's been on the force for six years."

"Yeah, as a dispatcher. What does she know about Homicide? Shit, I'm sorry I called you."

"No, you're not. I got Wilson off your ass. Besides, Sanchez really has got a nice pair of knockers. And she can write in English, too. Lopez can't. If it wasn't for being married, I'd trade you Lopez for Sanchez, but Marie would have a fit if I had myself a female partner."

"I thought Marie was liberated."

"She is, but I'm not."

"I'll lock your little thirty-two in your desk drawer."

"Keep it, old buddy. I'm not in any hurry for it."

CAPTAIN WILLIE BROWNLEY, wearing his navy blue uniform, complete with heavy jacket, sat behind a huge pile of paperwork in his glass-walled office. He gave Hoke a short lecture about hanging on to his new badge and .38 pistol this time.

"In my report, Hoke, I stressed the severity of the attack, and there'll be no problems with your record. The only problem you might have is with Ellita Sanchez. She told me that she would rather work with someone else instead of you. I get the idea she doesn't think you're macho enough—losing your gun and all."

"Jesus! Didn't you tell her the circumstances?"

"She knows, yes. But all the same, she wants to do well as a detective and asked me to put her with someone else. I think I straightened her out on that score, but I want you to know how she feels so you can win her over. She realizes that you're the sergeant, and she'll do whatever you tell her."

"I'm still going to be out for my two weeks' leave."

"I know. I'm moving Henderson and Lopez into the bullpen, and Sanchez into your office. Maybe she can catch up on some of your back paperwork."

"In that case, I'll see you in two weeks."

"Get rid of that beard before you come back. You look like that Puerto Rican actor, José Ferrer."

Hoke drove to the Trail Gun Shop and bought a new holster and a pair of handcuffs, charging them to his MasterCard, one that he had obtained from a bank in Chicago that issued them without a thorough credit check. It was the only charge card he had left, and he never missed sending the bank in Chicago the monthly payment of $10.

He then drove to the International Hotel, parked in the yellow zone, and looked for Pablo Lhosa. He showed Pablo his badge and ID, and asked him where they could go to talk. Pablo took him downstairs to the employees' locker room and opened his locker, which was secured with two padlocks. He took out a leather sports jacket and handed it to the detective.

"He left this jacket in his room," Pablo said. "He checked out of the hotel by telephone, paying by credit card. He was registered under the name of Herman T. Gotlieb, San Jose, California. The card, it turned out, was stolen. That's all I know. This jacket's too small for me, but it's expensive, and brand new. I want you to find him, lieutenant—"

"Sergeant."

"Yes, sir. This guy is scary. You should see his eyes—"

"I have."

"What I think, I think he's a hitman of some kind, imported from California."

"What gave you that idea?"

"Just the way he acts." Pablo shrugged. "I don't have no proof, but I know what a killer looks like. I served ten years in the National Guard in Nicaragua, and I've dealt with men who looked like him before."

"I'll find him. If you see him again, or if you can think of anything else, call me at my home address." Hoke gave Pablo one of his cards. "Let the phone ring for a long time. Sometimes no one's at the switchboard. But don't call me at the department for the next two weeks. Call me at home."

"Have you checked her apartment?" Pablo said. "They might be out there. A friend of mine checked once, but they weren't there. That doesn't mean that they won't be back. If you want to go out there, here's the keys to her apartment." Pablo took two keys off his ring and handed them to Hoke.

"How come you've got her apartment keys?"

"My friend gave 'em to me. He's got keys to everything in Miami. Here, why don't you keep the jacket, too? Except for the shoulders, you're both about the same size."

"Don't you want it? It's an expensive jacket."

"It won't fit me. I'm a forty-eight portly."

"Thanks. I'll find him, Pablo."

"It can't be too soon for me. I don't like violence of any kind."

"Yeah . . ." Hoke smiled. "That's why you left the Nicaraguan National Guard after only ten years."

HOKE USED THE pay phone in the lobby to call a friend of his in Records. He asked his friend to run a check on Herman T. Gotlieb in San Jose, California.

"How long will it take?" Hoke asked.

"It depends on a lot of things. Give me a couple of hours, okay?"

"I'll call you back, then. I don't know where I'll be two hours from now."

Hoke drove out to Kendall. He drew his pistol before he knocked on the door. When no one answered, he used the keys to get in. He looked through the rooms, but he couldn't tell for certain whether the pair was still living there or not. There were no men's clothes, but there was plenty of food in the refrigerator. The air conditioning was on, set for seventy-five degrees, and the brass bed in the master bedroom was unmade. There was a small jar of Oil of Olay and a can of Crisco on the bedside table. Except for two six-packs of San Miguel beer in the refrigerator, there was no liquor in the apartment. Hoke knew he shouldn't be in the apartment without a warrant, but he was positive that a fingerprint check on the jock would turn up a record in California. But how could he get a warrant? He couldn't tell a state attorney that he was positive it was Mendez who had attacked him. He had no tangible proof.

Hoke ate a bowl of chili and two tacos at the Taco Bell before going home. The hell with his diet. He needed to get his strength back. He took a shower and opened a package of Kools. The mentholated smoke tasted wonderful. A man would be a fool to give up smoking altogether. One cigarette, one, just one, once in a while, couldn't hurt.

He called his friend in Records. Herman T. Gotlieb, a mugging victim in San Francisco, had been found unconscious on Van Ness Avenue. He had been DOA when his body arrived by ambulance at the San Francisco General Hospital.

Hoke was not surprised by the information. He looked in the telephone book, noted the page and a half of Mendezes, and laughed. There were five Ramons and one Ramona, but it would be useless to call any of them because he knew that the man's name was not Mendez. All he knew for certain was that the man was armed and dangerous and that he somehow had to find him.

19

FOR SEVERAL DAYS after the fiasco at the 7-Eleven, Freddy was moody and inactive. His aching wrist gave him a good deal of pain, and although he didn't admit it to Susan, the nagging nature of the hurt made it difficult for him to sleep at night. They didn't have cable television, but he watched a Bowery Boys film festival on Channel 51 night after night, scowling at the commercials. Toward four A.M., when a faint Atlantic breeze wafted in through the open windows, Freddy would turn off the TV and fall into a restless sleep. Susan would be awakened by the sudden silence as the set clicked off. She would then tiptoe into the living room and cover him with a sheet.

After his shower and breakfast in the morning, Freddy sat on the back porch and looked through the screen at the lizards scurrying for survival in the back yard. There was a picket fence around the back yard, and a Barbados cherry hedge had been planted against the fence. Susan had neglected her small garden, and the tomato plants had withered. A dead coconut palm—killed by lethal yellow—arched up obscenely in the center of the yard. The fronds were gone, and the top of the tree was a shredded stub. Two lizards, in particular, Freddy noted, made the palm their home base. One, a hustler, darted here and there in search of mosquitoes, but the other one, the fatter of the two, moved rarely, except to inflate and deflate its mottled purple throat. When a mosquito came within range—zip! it was gone. In addition to being skinnier than the fatter, immobile lizard, the hustler lizard had lost the tip of its tail. Freddy thought there might be a lesson of some kind here for him to learn.

Freddy was reminded of Miles Darrell, an old fence he had worked with in Los Angeles. Miles would sometimes plan and bankroll a robbery and take half the profits. If the perpetrators were caught, Miles wrote off his investment and let it go at that. On the other hand, Miles was never a participant, and his careful plans usually worked out successfully. If the hooligans he recruited for a job were picked up, they accepted the bust stoically, and none of them ever informed on Miles. To do so would have been foolish. Even when convicted, the average stay in the joint was only two years, and a man knew when he got out he could count on a stake from Miles until he got back on his feet again.

Freddy had learned early in his career that it was best to work alone. If two or three men were in on a job and one was caught, the others would almost invariably be picked up later. Either deals were made by the man who was apprehended, or they would be picked up as the apprehended man's friends or acquaintances.

On the other hand, Miles, who had never been arrested, only got half the haul when a job was successful. The best method, Freddy concluded, was to plan and execute your own job. That way, no one could inform on you, and if you were successful, everything you got was yours. What he would like now was one large haul. One well-planned job, where the take would be large enough for several years of semiretirement living. Semi, not full retirement, because a man would have to put his hand in from time to time to keep from getting bored, but with enough money stashed away so that he could wait and pick and choose—like Miles. Miles had been a careful planner, and 90 percent of his jobs had been successful.

Perhaps Freddy had been too pessimistic about his life. He had figured, for as long as he could remember, that someday he would end up in prison for life, wandering around the yard as an old lag, muttering into a white beard and sniping cigarette butts.

But that didn't have to be—not if he could plan and execute one big job. Just one big haul . . .

But nothing came to him. He had no concrete ideas except for the germ, and the germ was that he had Sergeant Hoke Moseley's badge and ID. The badge was an automatic pass to free food and public transportation; it could also be used to bluff someone out of a considerable sum of cash. But who?

After lunch and a Darvon, Freddy usually napped on the webbed recliner on the back porch. He would awaken after an hour or two, covered with perspiration. He would then do a dozen one-arm pushups with his good arm and take a shower. He couldn't shave because of the cuts on his face. After a few days these cuts began to fester. They filled with yellow pus, and he had to pull off the colorful Band-Aids. He awoke one afternoon from his nap with a fever, and it made him dizzy when he tried to sit up in the recliner. He asked Susan to bring him some Bufferin and a pitcher of lemonade.

Susan brought the Bufferin and lemonade, and then left the house. She returned a few minutes later with Mrs. Damrosch, a short middle-aged woman who talked through a professional, meaningless, saleswoman's smile.

"Susan said you refused to see a doctor, and that you probably wouldn't let me take a look at you either. But you're wrong there, boy, I'm taking a look. I nursed my husband for three years before he died, and I can do the same for you—although you aren't going to die." She stuck a thermometer under his tongue and told him to close his mouth.

"Not bad," she said, when she removed the thermometer. "It's only one-oh-two, and we can get that down with some antibiotics. I've got a medicine cabinet full of 'em."

She slipped her glasses down her nose and peered into his face, still smiling and shaking her head. "Some of those punctures've still got glass in 'em. I'll go home and be right back."

"Go with her, Susie," Freddy said, "and make sure she doesn't call a doctor."

Mrs. Damrosch had no intention of calling a doctor. She returned with medicines, unguents, a razor blade, and tweezers. She crosscut each of the punctures in his face with the razor blade and removed bits of glass with her tweezers, telling Freddy in her cheerful voice that it would hurt. She also removed the crude stitches Freddy had taken to replace his eyebrow. She made some butterfly adhesive patches and replaced them on the gaping places that had not, as yet, grown back together. She used two more butterfly patches on the two deepest wounds on his face but said it would be best just to let the others drain.

She and Susan helped Freddy walk to the bedroom. Edna Damrosch poured Freddy a glass of gin, made him drink most of it, and then sponged his muscular body with a mixture of water and rubbing alcohol. When she removed Freddy's jeans, Susan took the sponge away from her and said:

"I'll take care of that part."

Edna laughed. "I would too if I were you!"

This drastic treatment, in addition to penicillin tablets every four hours, broke Freddy's fever. By noon the next day he was sitting up in bed and eating a roast beef sandwich. He remained in the air-conditioned bedroom for two more days at Edna's insistence, then felt strong enough to take a long, soaking bath.

When he looked at his face in the mirror, he could barely discern the scabbed crisscrosses beneath his beard. The thick stubble, a quarter of an inch long in some places, was a mixture of blond, brown, and jet-black whiskers—not matching his burnished yellow hair in the slightest. If he was careful he could probably shave, but he decided to keep the incipient beard. It would cover the scars somewhat, and it might be a way to change his appearance. By now the Miami police were looking for him, but they weren't looking for a man with a blond, brown, and blackish beard. The beard, together with the healing scabs, made his face itch, but he was determined not to scratch his neck or face. His refusal to scratch caused jerky tics to develop on both cheeks, but at least the tics relieved the itching. The following day he took a hammer to the cast on his arm. His wrist was stiff and slightly atrophied, so while he watched TV he squeezed a tennis ball to strengthen his wrist and fingers.

THREE WEEKS AFTER the accident at the 7-Eleven, Freddy put on his Italian suit, took the car keys, and drove into downtown Miami. He had studied the Yellow Pages and the ads in the *Miami Herald*, and he had a tentative plan. He cased three different coin dealers before picking a major one on Flagler Street. Flagler was Miami's main street, and the downtown stretch of Flagler was one-way, but just around the corner on Miami Avenue there was a yellow loading zone. If Susan pulled into the loading zone and sat in the car, a mere thirty yards around the corner from the coin dealer's, she could probably stay there for a half-hour or more before some cop came along and told her to move. The coin dealer, a man named Ruben Wulgemuth, had a reinforced steel door to his shop, and there was a circular, revolving bulletproof window in the wall beside the door. To transact business with the dealer, patrons outside on the sidewalk placed their coins or whatever into the drawer of the revolving window. Except for his regular customers, Wulgemuth didn't let anyone inside his shop. But Freddy knew how to get inside.

Over the asparagus that night, Freddy explained Susan's

duties to her. Freddy had never eaten asparagus before, nor had he ever tried hollandaise sauce, but he liked it a lot, especially with the center-cut ham steak and scalloped potatoes au gratin. Susan, whose part in the plan was minimal but essential, was apprehensive because Freddy did not feel that it was necessary to tell her what he was going to do.

"I know you don't like questions, Junior," she said, "but I want to do it right."

"I don't mind questions," he said, appropriating Susan's uneaten asparagus. "I just don't like dumb questions."

"You haven't told me what's going down. If I knew what you were going to do, it would help me do what you want me to do."

"No, it wouldn't. All you have to do is park in the yellow zone and keep the engine running. Nothing could be simpler. I'll get out of the car and do my business with the coin dealer. If a cop or a meter maid comes along, tell them that you're waiting for your husband to finish a transaction with the coin shop around the corner. The cops know Wulgemuth does business with people on the street, and that's a legitimate reason to park in a loading zone. They may make you move anyway, but then you just drive around the block as fast as you can without breaking the speed limit and park there again. If you're forced to move, lean on your horn with a long two-minute blast as you come by the shop. I'll be inside, but I'll hear you."

"It'll only take a few seconds to pass the shop, so how can I blow the horn for two minutes?"

"Start blowing when you turn the corner onto Flagler, and keep the horn on all the way up the block after you pass the shop. That's what I mean by a two-minute blast. Think, Susan, think. If someone looks at you funny for holding down the horn, pretend like it's stuck."

"Like this?" Susan dropped her jaw, made an *O* with her mouth, and opened her eyes wide.

"That's it!" Freddy laughed.

"You laughed! I don't remember you laughing before, not even at TV."

"You never did anything funny before. I don't laugh at TV because it isn't real."

"All right. So what I do is park there and keep the engine running. If nobody makes me move, I just wait for you. When you get back into the car I drive down to Biscayne, take the MacArthur Causeway, and pull into the parking lot on Watson Island."

"The Japanese Garden parking lot. We'll stay parked in the lot until it gets dark, and then we'll drive back here to Dania by way of Miami Beach. The Japanese Garden has been vandalized, so they've closed it for repairs. No one parks in the Garden lot now, except for a few fishermen in the daytime and some lovers at night. So, if we aren't followed, it'll be easy to hide out there all afternoon until it gets dark. You'd better pack some kind of lunch and a thermos with iced tea."

"Suppose we're followed—and why would anybody want to follow us?"

"Don't worry about it. If we're followed, I'll deal with it, but we won't be. When you ask why, you're asking another dumb question."

"I'm sorry."

"What's for dessert?"

"Sweet potato pie."

"I've never had that before."

"It tastes like punkin pie. If I didn't tell you, you'd probably think it was punkin pie, but sweet potato's better."

"I'll try it. I like pumpkin pie."

"You want whipped cream on it?"

"Of course."

After dinner, Susan drove them to the Dania jai alai fronton. While she was buying the tickets, Freddy scouted the parking lot and unbolted a Kansas license plate from a Ford Escort. He locked the plate into his trunk to exchange for the TransAm plate when they got home. Freddy watched the first game and decided he didn't know enough about the game or the players to make an intelligent wager.

Susan, however, by betting on the Basque players who had the first name of Jesus—there were three that night— won $212.35.

20

HOKE STILL HAD Bill Henderson's .32 automatic pistol when he left the police station. He had meant to lock it in Henderson's desk drawer, but when he had seen Ellita Sanchez sitting at the double desk in the little office, he changed his mind. He had got a good look at Sanchez, however, and noticed that she did indeed have large breasts, although they were disguised somewhat by her loose silk blouse and the large silk bow that was tied under her throat. Her black hair was bobbed the way they used to cut the hair of little Chinese girls. The back of her slender white neck looked as if it had been shaved. She wore blue-tinted glasses, and she was frowning, with tightly pursed lips, as she read through a file. She tapped the glass top of the desk absently with a yellow pencil. If he went into the office, she would surely ask him some questions about the paperwork. Sanchez was a formidable-looking woman, and Hoke did not relish the idea of working with her, or as Brownley had put it, "winning her over." So he had left the station without talking to her.

Hoke thought about Ellita Sanchez now, however, as he sat in his room, trying to figure out his next move. Whatever he did, he would have to be careful. He didn't want to involve Sergeant Wilson, the Vice cop, nor did he want to make a legal mistake of some kind that would result in bail or a quick release for Mendez. He had to get that man off the street forever.

There was no doubt in Hoke's mind that Mendez had mugged the unfortunate Gotlieb, whose credit card he had then stolen and used at the International Hotel, but he had no proof of the mugging, nor could he get a warrant on the strength of how he happened to feel about it. And there was always the possibility that Mendez had bought the stolen credit card from someone else. For fifty bucks apiece, a man could buy all the stolen cards he wanted at the downtown bus station.

Hoke went to the desk and poured an overflowing jigger of Early Times into his tooth glass. Too much. He poured part of it back into the bottle. His hands shook a little, and he spilled part of his drink. He could hear his heart beat. The more he thought about Mendez, the more afraid he was. This was not paranoia. When a man has beaten you badly and you know that he can do it to you again, a wholesome fear is a sign of intelligence.

There was only one thing to do, and that was to find Mendez and follow him. Then, if he could find his gun and badge on the bastard, he could bring him in for assault or attempted murder. At the very least, Mendez could be held for a few days without bail, long enough to run a fingerprint check out to California to see what they had on him. If the man had a record, and Hoke was certain he had one, the chances were good that he was wanted in California, too. If he wasn't on the run from California, why had he come to Miami?

Hoke had calmed down a little. The drink had helped so much he poured another one. His hands were steady now. Hoke lit a Kool and picked up the phone. After he listened to it buzz at the switchboard fifteen or sixteen times, he lost count. Finally Eddie Cohen answered the phone.

"Desk."

"Eddie, this is Sergeant Moseley. Dial my number at the police station for me, will you, please?"

Ellita Sanchez picked up the phone before it could ring a second time. "Homicide. Detective Sanchez."

"Hello, Sanchez. This is your new partner, Sergeant Hoke Moseley. I was in earlier today to see Captain Brownley, but you looked so busy I didn't want to bother you. Anyway, Captain Brownley—"

"Who? You want Captain Brownley?"

"No." Hoke hesitated. Sanchez didn't have much of an accent, but Hoke realized that he was talking too fast for her to follow him. "This is Sergeant Moseley. I am your new partner."

"Yes, sergeant."

"We're going to be working together. You and me. Captain Brownley told me today. When I came to see him."

"Yes."

"I want you to do a couple of things for me."

"What?"

"You can probably handle it all with a few phone calls. If not, take a car and visit Florida Power and Light, and the phone company. The water department, too. Perhaps you should check the water company first."

"What case is this one? Should I not read the file first?"

"No, that won't be necessary. Just take down this information as I give it to you."

"Captain Brownley told me you wouldn't be back to work for two weeks. If you're on sick leave, why are we working on a new case? And why are you withholding information from me when I'm your partner? I don't understand this at all. So, before I do anything for you, Sergeant Moseley, I'm going to check with Captain Brownley to see if it's all right. The way I—"

"Shut up." Hoke's deep voice dropped an octave with anger.

"What?"

"I said shut up. Now listen, Sanchez, because I don't

173

want to repeat myself. We are indeed new partners, but I am the senior partner, and a sergeant. You're the junior partner, and you're not a detective yet. So far you're a dispatcher with a Latin name. And because you have a Latin name, you've been given a chance to work with me as a detective.

"Luckily for you, you've been assigned to a patient, understanding Homicide detective who'll take the time to explain the facts of life to you. *If*, under any circumstances, I give you an order, or a request, or a suggestion, and you go over my head to check it out with Captain Brownley or go to anyone else who happens to be my superior, I guarantee you that you'll be lucky to become a dispatcher again.

"In fact, you'll never see the inside of a police station again. I'll see to it that you're assigned permanently to the night shift at the Orange Bowl, from midnight to eight A.M. So if you don't want to spend the rest of your police career checking the locks on vending machines, get a pencil and a piece of paper and follow my instructions. Do you understand, or do I have to run it by you again?"

"I understand, sergeant."

"Good. Check with the water department, the F.P. and L., and Ma Bell. And see if anyone named Waggoner or Mendez—W-A-G-G-O-N-E-R, and you can spell Mendez—put down a new deposit in the last three weeks. Water, Florida Power, and phone company. Just during the last three weeks. If you don't get a list of names and addresses from these three, make another call to the Public Gas Company, just in case there's an outside tank. Any questions?"

"No. I got it."

"Then call me back here at the Eldorado Hotel by five today on what you've found out. Let the phone ring at least twenty times before you hang up. The man at the desk is hard of hearing. If I don't hear from you by five, I'll call you at your desk by five-thirty. Got that?"

"Yes."

"Till five, then."

174

"Yes."

Hoke got up from the rolltop desk and crossed to the side table by the Victorian armchair where he had left his bottle of Early Times.

That wasn't exactly what Captain Brownley had in mind, Hoke thought, when he said I would have to win Ellita Sanchez over. By the time I finish this drink, she'll be in Brownley's office. By the time I start to pour another, she'll be explaining to Willie Brownley how I have been discriminating against her for being a Latin, first, and for being a woman, second. She'll tell Brownley about my threat, and I'll have to make it good. Whether there are enough people left in the department who owe me enough favors to send Sanchez to the Orange Bowl is a moot question. But I can get her out of Homicide. That much I know I can do. Vice! Sergeant Wilson. Sergeant Wilson threw my teeth out the window. He owes me for that. I can get Wilson to ask for her in Vice. A few months of trapping johns on 79th Street will be good training for Sanchez, and after she works for a mean prick like Wilson for a couple of weeks she will surely wish to hell she had done what kindly old Hoke Moseley asked her to do . . .

Hoke finished his drink. He lit another cigarette, smoked it down to the cork tip, and put it out in the ashtray with the Hotel Fontainebleau logo. There was no telephone call from Captain Brownley.

AT FOUR-THIRTY P.M. the phone woke Hoke from his nap. Sanchez had a list of names and addresses for him. There were two Mendezes, one Wagner, one Wegner, and one Susan Waggoner. Susan Waggoner, however, was not in Dade County. She had put down deposits for water, electricity, gas, and a telephone in Dania, which was right over the county line in Broward County.

Hoke hadn't told Sanchez to check in Broward County, but he had, apparently, frightened her into using initiative.

21

THE RAIN BEGAN to fall lightly at four-thirty A.M., but by six, when the lightning flashed and the thunder rumbled, passing over Dade County from the Everglades, the rain came down in torrents. Hoke cursed the rain and rolled up the window to avoid getting drenched. The windows steamed almost immediately, and he had to wipe the inside of the windshield with his handkerchief.

Hoke had been parked under a cluster of sea-grape trees since four A.M. The overhanging branches with their huge leaves concealed most of his car from Susan Waggoner's little house a hundred yards away on the other side of the street. The rain, as he thought about it, would make tailing easier. He didn't know whether Mendez was in the house with Susan or not, but he was certain that she would lead him to Mendez if he followed her long enough.

When the lights in the house went on at six-fifteen, Hoke was more than a little surprised. He hadn't expected the girl to get up so early. Hoke took a leak in the coffee can, replaced the lid, and placed the warm can on the floor in front of the passenger's seat. He wanted another cigarette, but he wouldn't light one now because the girl might see the glow. The girl was his only lead to Mendez, and he didn't intend to take any chances. The white TransAm, with its Kansas license plate, would be easy to follow, whereas his own beatup Pontiac blended right in with the thousands of dented cars on Miami's highways. No, the only thing that bothered Hoke was the actual apprehension of Ramon Mendez, but he would be able to handle that when the time came . . .

FREDDY AWOKE AT six, went to the bathroom, showered, and then shook Susan awake. Freddy was pleased by the rain and asked Susan how long she thought it would last. Susan, who was bustling in the kitchen preparing a large breakfast, went to the window and looked out.

"This is the tail end of the hurricane season, and we always get a lot of rain. It could last three or four days, or it may pass over in two or three hours. From the looks of the sky, I'd say all day."

Susan ladled chipped beef and peppery milk gravy over six buttered toast points. She set the plate in front of Freddy and stepped back as he forked a huge mouthful and chewed with his eyes closed.

"This is good SOS," he said. "But you should've fixed home fries to go with it. SOS tastes better over potatoes than it does on toast. That way, you can eat the toast separately with a little marmalade. This gravy's so thick I can hardly taste the butter on the toast."

"It won't take a minute to fix some home fries, if that's what you want. There's a cold baked potato in the fridge, and I can slice it up—"

"No, this is okay. I meant for next time. I like a big breakfast when I go out on a job. Gives a man energy."

"How's your wrist?"

Freddy got up from the table, dropped to the floor, and did a one-arm pushup with his bad arm. "That's one," he said, wincing as he sat at the table again. "Tomorrow I'll try for two."

"Does it still hurt, I mean?"

"A little, when I do pushups. But I don't think it was ever broken, or it wouldn't've healed by now. Probably just a bad sprain."

"I guess this rain don't make no nevermind to your plans, does it?"

"It helps us, that's all, by cutting down the visibility. Did you fix the lunch yet?"

"Tunafish sandwiches, what's left of the vinegar pie, some apples and bananas. And two bags of Doritos. There's tea in the thermos, and a six-pack of Dr. Pepper. I already put the stuff in the car."

Freddy nodded, and poured another cup of coffee. "That's plenty. We probably won't be hungry anyway, after this big breakfast, but after you've been sitting in a car for a few hours, eating gives you something to do. You'd better put an empty coffee can in the car, too."

"What for?"

"Sometime, Susie, before you ask a stupid question, why don't you think for a minute? Where d'you think the iced tea and those Dr. Peppers are gonna go?"

"The can's to pee in?"

"See how easy it is?"

Susan frowned. The two little lines between her eyes deepened, and she compressed her lips.

"If something's bothering you," Freddy said, "spit it out. I don't like the way you're behaving this morning."

"What you're making me do isn't fair."

"How's that?"

"The man's the man, and the woman's a woman in a marriage. You're supposed to go out and bring in the money, and I stay home and keep house. It isn't fair to make me help you do whatever it is you're going to do, and I'm scared."

"What're you afraid of? All you've got to do is park the car in the yellow zone and wait for me to come back."

"I think you're going to do something illegal, and if I'm helping you, I could get into trouble, too. I gave up a promising college career to marry you and take care of the house and all, and I shouldn't have to—"

"Who's been filling your head with all this shit? Edna Damrosch, next door?"

"Nobody has to tell me when to be scared. I know enough to be scared when I'm doing something I'm not supposed to do."

"So if I tell you what I'm going to do, you won't be scared, is that it?"

"That's right."

"I'm going to rob this coin dealer, a guy named Wulgemuth. The coin collection I'm taking with me will help me get inside his shop. It's worth a couple of hundred bucks, or more, but I'll leave it there when I take the man's cash. He's got his own safe, and he deals in gold and big money, so his safe'll have a lot of cash in it. No telling how much. That's what I plan to get. So now you can relax."

"Relax? I'm more scared then ever."

"See what I mean? That's why I didn't tell you before. I knew you'd act this way. Just keep in mind how simple your part is. You park and drive the car. There's nothing to wet your pants about."

"And I won't get into trouble?"

"Not a chance. This job is foolproof. I've checked it out from every angle. When it's all over we'll have so much money I'll take you on a Caribbean cruise."

"Why can't you do it alone?"

"Because I can't take a chance and have the car towed away while I'm in the store. You've got to be in it."

Susan nodded and started to gather the dishes.

"Leave the dishes. You can do them later tonight, after we come home."

THE HEAVY RAIN and several accidents on the highway had slowed traffic on the Dixie Highway to a crawl, and Hoke Moseley had no trouble following the TransAm.

Although it was after nine A.M., the bruised sky and the heavy rain made it seem like early dawn. Impatient drivers with their lights and wipers on inched along the flooded streets, crowding over toward the center line. Some honked their horns just to be honking their horns. When Susan sped up to race through a yellow light, Freddy told her to slow down.

"There's no hurry," he said. "It doesn't make any real difference when we get there. Even the noon hour would be okay. I've checked twice, and the man is alone in his shop and doesn't close up for lunch. Probably brings it with him."

"I'm sorry. It's just that I'm still scared and a little nervous. Besides, if you stop for a yellow light in Miami you get rear-ended."

"I can't understand why you're scared. All you've got to do is park in the yellow zone, and——"

"I know all that! I'm going to be all right."

The yellow loading zone on Miami Avenue was vacant. It was long enough for three compact cars or for one car and a full-size truck. After Susan pulled into the loading zone, Freddy told her to back up to the end of the zone so she couldn't be blocked from behind. "That still leaves room for a truck to park in front of you in case somebody needs to unload something for that *ropa* store."

Next to the Cuban clothing store there was a narrow shop with a stuffed llama in the window. The store claimed to sell genuine Peruvian imports, but the floor beneath the llama was layered with Timex watches and zircon rings in black velvet boxes. On the corner was a small Cuban cafeteria with a Formica counter to serve customers on the sidewalk.

Freddy held the coin case in his lap. He took out his .38 pistol, checked it, and then put the pistol back in his right coat pocket.

"You—you aren't going to shoot Mr. Wulgemuth, are you?" Susan said, licking her thin lips.

"Not unless I have to," Freddy said. "But sometimes,"

180

Freddy shrugged, "they make you do it." Freddy smiled like a butcher's dog. "Like the time I broke your brother's finger. He irritated me, and I had to break it."

"You killed Martin?"

"I didn't kill anybody. I broke his fucking finger, that's all. And if you force me into it, by not doing exactly what I tell you, I'll break your skinny neck."

Freddy got out of the car and ordered two café Cubanos at the counter. He downed his quickly and took the other one, in its one-ounce paper cup, back to the car. Susan rolled down the window, and he handed her the coffee. Her hand trembled so much she spilled most of the coffee on her jeans. There was a rim of white around her lips. Freddy shook his head impatiently.

"D'you want another cup?"

Susan shook her head. Her knuckles holding the wheel were white.

"All right, then. Stay awake, keep the engine running, and I should be back in about ten minutes." Carrying the coin case in his left hand, Freddy walked away from the car.

HOKE WAS STOPPED by the red light. Susan, in the TransAm, had made it across just in time. Hoke watched her pull into the yellow loading zone on Miami Avenue and then back up to the end of the zone. Except for the spaces in front of her TransAm, there were no other vacant spaces on the street. A horn honked behind him. Hoke rolled down the window and waved the driver around. The man had to back up before he could pull forward again to get around Hoke's car. He cursed Hoke and shook his fist as he roared by.

Hoke watched Mendez get out of the car and buy coffee at the cafeteria. He took a cup back to the car. Hoke wondered if that was why they had stopped—to get a fucking cup of Cuban coffee? Another car pulled up behind Hoke and stopped. The light was green again, and the driver leaned on her horn. Hoke waved her around.

When Hoke looked back at the TransAm, he noticed

Mendez turning the corner onto Flagler. As Mendez disappeared into the rain, the TransAm pulled away from the curb, with its tires squealing on the wet street, and raced down Miami Avenue. Hoke followed the TransAm, thinking, he's going to buy something on Flagler, and she's going to circle the block to pick him up so he won't get wet. But Hoke had guessed wrong. That's why a man needed a partner. If he had had Bill Henderson with him—or even Ellita Sanchez—she could have followed Susan, and he could have gone after Mendez on foot.

When Hoke realized that the TransAm had got into the lane leading to the I-95 overpass, he switched lanes, bluffed his way into the outside lane, and made a left turn at First Street. He drove down a block, made another left, and finally got back on Flagler. The cars were barely moving and Hoke was caught by two red lights, but he inched along Flagler, watching the pedestrians make short dashes from one overhanging awning to the next. There was a crowd of South Americans with shopping bags standing in the arcade that catered to Venezuelans and Colombians. Hoke stopped completely to look them over. Mendez, in his light suit, would stand out among all those foreigners in funereal black. Hoke took out his pistol and laid it on the seat beside him. He looked at the empty bracket from which his radio had been stolen, and swore. Horns honked behind him, and he moved forward again. His only chance was to spot Mendez in the street, and that seemed damned unlikely. Deep down, way down there in the pit of his stomach, he hoped he wouldn't find him.

FREDDY'S HAIR WAS wet and the shoulders of his gray silk suitcoat were soaked through by the time he rounded the corner to Flagler and reached the window of Wulgemuth's Coin Exchange. Freddy pressed the buzzer beside the window and smiled when he saw Wulgemuth's alert face behind the glass. The coin expert was in his early fifties but looked older because of his bald head, which was encircled by a clipped wreath of stubby white hair above his ears. His bulbous nose and his sunken cheeks were pitted with old acne scars.

"I'm a police officer," Freddy said into the recessed microphone. "Turn the window."

The bulletproof window revolved. Freddy placed the cowhide coin case in the drawer, and dropped his ID card and badge, still in its leather holder, on top of the case. The window revolved and Wulgemuth's face disappeared.

There were more people shopping on Flagler than Freddy had expected to see on such a miserable, rainy day, but most of them, Freddy supposed, were used to the rain. The rain was warm, and in places the sidewalk steamed. The temperature, despite the rain, was eighty-two degrees, as Freddy could see by the lighted digital clock on the bank tower a block away. The time was 10:04. The time and temperature flashed off, and were replaced by an aqueous message in dotted green lights:

THE AMERICAN WAY
IS OUR IRA

The message puzzled Freddy. What was an IRA? He heard the window revolve. The badge and the ID were in the drawer, but not the coin case. Wulgemuth's face was in the window again. "What's your business, sergeant?"

"Police business," Freddy said. "I've been trying to get a line on these stolen coins, and I've got some other things to ask you about. Open the door." Freddy took his badge out of the drawer.

The face disappeared. A buzzer on the door lock sounded, and Freddy turned the knob as the door lock was released. The buzzing stopped as he stepped inside.

"Shut the door!" Wulgemuth called from the back of the shop.

Freddy closed the door with his hip. Wulgemuth had the coin case open on the counter at the end of the narrow shop.

"These coins were stolen, you say?"

"Yeah. I brought them down from the property room. We picked them up on a fencing bust, and we figured if we could get a line on the owner we could find out something more on the burglars. Is this a valuable collection, or not?"

Wulgemuth shrugged. "What you're talking about here, sergeant, is intrinsic value. That's what I deal in. It's worth what someone wants to pay for it, and that's probably a lot more than its face value. This is by no means a rare collection, even though a cursory look shows that all the coins are in pretty fair condition."

"Did you ever see it before?"

"As a collection, no, but I've seen a lot like it. What happened to your eye, anyway?"

"Car accident."

"You oughta sue the doctor who sewed you up. You could make a bundle."

"He said it would look okay once it scarred over."

"He lied. Anyway, this isn't my coin case, either."

Freddy closed the lid on the case, and snapped the two hasp locks closed. "I'll try another dealer. Can you show me one of your coin cases? I'd like to see how different yours are from this one."

"I don't have any on hand, not right now."

"Not even in your safe?"

"None for silver dollars."

"Who else sells cowhide cases like this one, then?"

"You're on the wrong track, sergeant. All the trade magazines advertise cases like this. You can order coin cases by mail, from cheap canvas jobs to custom-made ostrich with your initials in gold."

"I see."

"How come a Homicide detective's so interested in tracing stolen property? Is there a murder involved in this collection?"

"That's confidential, Mr. Wulgemuth. I'm also checking out your place here for security. We've had a tip, you see, and we're thinking about putting a stakeout in here. Someone—we don't know who—has been hitting coin dealers."

"You're telling me! D'you know how many times I've been robbed? Before I put in that window, I was hit three times in one month! But I don't need any stakeouts now."

"Why not?" Freddy smiled, and reached into his jacket pocket for his pistol. His fingers closed over the cross-hatched grip.

"Because of Pedro." Wulgemuth turned his head. "Pedro!"

The door in the back opened with a bang. A short, wide-shouldered, dark-haired man came through the doorway. His double-barreled shotgun was pointed at Freddy's chest. His dark, serious face was expressionless.

"He's been watching you all the time through the peephole in the door." Wulgemuth laughed. "It's okay, Pedro. This is Detective Sergeant Moseley. He's with the police department."

Pedro lowered his shotgun and turned toward the back door. As he turned, Freddy pulled out his .38 and shot him in the back. Pedro fell, face down, through the open door to the back storeroom. The shotgun clattered on the terrazzo floor but did not go off. Freddy was still looking down at Pedro, deciding whether to fire another shot, when Wulgemuth with a sweeping motion brought up a machete from beneath the counter. In a wide arc, he brought it down on Freddy's left hand, which was resting on the coin case. Freddy's little finger, the ring finger, and the middle finger were lopped off cleanly at their second joints. The force of the downward swing drove the blade into the leather of the case. Freddy shot Wulgemuth in the face. The bullet made a round hole just below his nose. He fell back with a gurgling sound, dead before his bald head hit the terrazzo floor.

For a long moment, Freddy looked without comprehension at the exposed and bloody bones of his left hand. The hand was numb at first, and then he felt a jolt that raced back and forth from his hand to his elbow. The stumps of his fingers were bleeding, but not as much as he would have expected them to bleed. He wrapped his handkerchief around his wounded hand, lifted the hinged Formica lid, and went behind the counter. He tried to open the six-foot wall safe, but the combination safe was closed and locked. He opened the cash drawer behind the counter. There were several bills in various denominations, as well as change in separate compartments. Freddy dropped his pistol back into his jacket pocket and scooped up the stack of tens and twenties. He turned over Wulgemuth's body with his good hand and took the coin dealer's wallet out of his hip pocket. Freddy stuffed the wallet and the bills into his inside jacket pocket and went to the front door.

He couldn't open it. He returned to the counter and stuck a paper clip into the door's buzzer release so he could get out. He shut the heavy door behind him as he left, and the door lock continued to buzz. Anyone could walk in now, and the first one to do so would discover the bodies. But he still had plenty of time. Freddy put his wounded hand into his trousers pocket and walked through the rain to the corner, fighting an urge to run.

There was a white Toyota half-ton truck in the yellow loading zone, but Susan and the white TransAm were gone.

Freddy made an abrupt about-face and started back toward Flagler. Perhaps it had been a mistake to tell Susie that he had broken Martin's finger. Anyone else might have questioned him about it; it was so unlikely to meet a brother and a sister in two different places on the same day in a strange town. But she had believed him because he had never lied to her before. He hadn't told her much of anything about himself, so there had been no need to lie. But her whining had pissed him off. Of course, she might have been forced to move by a meter maid. In that case she would be coming up Flagler by now and he could wave her down from the curb. In the pelting rain, he stared down the street at the crawling cars on Flagler. A battered Pontiac Le Mans stopped suddenly in the middle of the street.

Freddy and Hoke recognized each other at the same time. Hoke stuck his left arm through the open window and pointed his pistol at Freddy.

"Freeze! Police!" Hoke shouted.

There were three women with umbrellas on the sidewalk. Freddy stepped in among them, gave Hoke the finger, and ran. He knew that the cop wouldn't fire into the pedestrians. For a cop to use deadly force, his life had to be threatened. Freddy crossed the street against the red light, dodging the slowly moving cars, ignoring their horns, and trotted up Flagler toward Burdine's Department Store. He looked back once as he entered the store, but no one was following him. He walked briskly through the store, past the men's clothing section, and then took the back exit to First Street. There were more than a dozen people in a ragged half-formed line as the Hialeah Metro bus pulled up to the bus stop. Freddy pushed through the umbrellas to the head of the line, and as the door opened, entered the bus and flashed his badge in the driver's face.

"Police," he said. "I'm looking for a nigger with a radio."

The bus driver jerked his thumb. "There's three of 'em back there."

The bus was crowded. Every seat was filled, and Freddy had to elbow his way through the standing passengers. There were three black men with radios in the long back seat, and they had spread out so no one else could sit down. But only one man, with a khaki knitted watch cap pulled low over his forehead, had his radio turned on. He was bobbing his head to a reggae beat. Freddy showed the man his badge and told him to turn off his radio. Sullenly, the man turned down the volume a fraction of an inch.

"I said, 'Off!'"

The man apparently saw something in Freddy's eyes. The radio was clicked off, and several nearby passengers clapped their hands. After three blocks, Freddy pulled the cord, and the driver stopped at the corner. As Freddy pushed through the back doors, the radio started again.

HOKE GOT OUT of the car and watched Mendez dodge nimbly between the cars as he ran across the intersection and up the crowded sidewalk. Hoke lost sight of him when he slipped in front of two elderly women with shielding umbrellas. Hoke looked around for a uniformed policeman. There was usually a traffic officer on this corner, but there was no cop here today. He was probably inside somewhere, drinking coffee and staying out of the rain. The stalled traffic behind Hoke's car honked ominously. He couldn't leave the car in the middle of the intersection and run after his quarry. Hoke got back into his car, scanning the sidewalk as he picked up some speed, but he didn't have much hope. The man could have zipped into any one of thirty stores, including Woolworth's and Burdine's.

Susan, Hoke figured, was taking the I-95 Expressway back to Dania, which would get her home twice as fast as a trip back to Dania on South Dixie. Hoke would have to go back to Dania, question her, and then if she refused to tell him where Mendez was, could threaten to book her on a solicitation charge. He could threaten her, but he couldn't pick her up. Dania was in Broward County, and Hoke had no jurisdiction in Broward County.

At Sixth Street, Hoke turned right and found a parking space in front of a cigar store. He went inside, showed the man behind the counter his badge, and asked for the phone. The phone was on the wall behind the dealer's back, but the receiver was on a long cord. The dealer, a white-haired Latin with a hoarse voice, handed the receiver to Hoke.

"You tell me number. I dial. No one can come behind counter. I dial."

Hoke gave the man his office number. Ellita Sanchez answered the phone.

"This is Sergeant Moseley, Sanchez. Is Bill Henderson around?"

"He was in earlier, but he's not here now. I think he went downstairs for coffee."

"You don't happen to know any cops in Dania, do you?"

"No. I've never even been to Dania."

"That's okay. I want you to get a message to Sergeant Henderson. Tell him that I need a cop from Broward County to meet me at two-four-six Poinciana, in Dania. You remember—the address of Susan Waggoner in Dania you got for me yesterday."

"I've got a cousin on the force in Hollywood. I could call him, if you want."

"He'll do, but I'd rather have a Dania cop. Talk to Henderson first. He'll know what to do. But if you can't find Henderson, call your cousin in Hollywood. Tell Henderson that I've got a good chance to pick up Mendez."

"You can't arrest anybody in Broward County."

"I know it, Sanchez. That's why I want a cop from Dania, and I don't know anyone there and it would all be too complicated to explain to anyone there over the phone. So just tell Henderson what I've told you. D'you understand?"

"I'll go down to the cafeteria right now and look for him."

"Good girl." Hoke handed the receiver back to the white-haired man. The man smiled and held up two fingers as he took the receiver. "Last month at Dania I hit two trifectas."

"Wonderful," Hoke said. "Thanks for the phone."

There was a tiny cafeteria next to the cigar store. Hoke ordered a double espresso, drank it, and then bought two Jamaican hot meat patties to eat in the car on his way to Dania.

22

As the taillights of the Metrobus disappeared into the rain, Freddy walked through an A-1 Park-and-Lock lot and into an Eckerd's drugstore. He bought a roll of gauze and a roll of adhesive tape and left the store. He kept his injured hand in his trousers pocket, and flexed his thumb and forefinger. They responded in time with the shooting pains to his elbow. The hand was no longer numb, but the pain wasn't steady. It flashed and flickered off and on like a broken neon sign.

A bearded man in his early thirties wearing a dirty yellow T-shirt stood under a ragged awning in front of a boarded-up storefront. He was drinking from a bottle in a brown paper bag.

"Are you drunk?" Freddy asked him.

The man shook his head. "Not yet."

"I'll give you five bucks to do something for me."

"Okay."

"Bind up my hand."

Freddy handed the bearded man the sack from Eckerd's, moved back into the recessed doorway, and took his wounded hand out of his pocket. He unwrapped the sticky handkerchief.

The derelict put down his bottle carefully by the wall and took the gauze and adhesive tape out of the sack. Freddy held out his hand and the man shook his head and clucked.

"Nasty," he said.

He wrapped Freddy's hand tightly with the gauze, including the unimpaired forefinger, but left the thumb free. The man's fingers were shaky but functional.

"You can't do nothin' without your thumb," he explained.

He used all the gauze and all the tape because he didn't have a knife to cut off the excess, but the wrapping was so tight it looked like a professional job.

"That'll do her till you get to a doctor."

Freddy gave the man $10.

"This is a ten," the man said.

Freddy shrugged. "Five's for the bandage job, and the other five's for getting me a cab."

"I'll be right back." The man hesitated. "Don't let anybody touch my bottle." Limping slightly in his huaraches, the man hurried toward Flagler in the rain. The rain had a steady beat to it now, as though it would last forever.

Freddy picked up the bottle and took a long swig from it. Muscatel wine. Sweet and fruity, and devoid of subtlety. Freddy drank the rest of it anyway and put the bottle down by the wall again. The sweet wine didn't lessen the pain in his hand. He needed whiskey for that, but the Darvon he had back at the house in Dania would help more than whiskey. He regretted his hasty retreat from the coin exchange. He should have scooped up the stubs of his fingers he left behind. The cops would get his fingerprints from them. Shit. Murder One. The time had come to get the hell out of Miami. He would tell Susie to drive him to Okeechobee. She undoubtedly knew a doctor up there, and after he got his hand fixed up they could head north. They could hole up along the way in one of those Days Inns that dotted I-95 in every small Florida town. Then, when his hand had healed, he would decide what to do next. Maybe

191

they could fly out to Vegas. There was a lot going on in Vegas.

A Veteran's Cab pulled up to the curb. The derelict got out, and Freddy handed him another $5. "I finished off your bottle," Freddy said. "Buy yourself another."

"That's all right. Thanks a lot. I didn't mean you, anyway. I meant if somebody else came along. Thanks!"

Freddy got into the cab. He began to sweat, and a wave of nausea swept over him as his stomach cramped. He leaned forward and vomited on the floor. It all came up, filling the cab with the aromas of chipped beef, milk gravy, and muscatel wine.

"That's gonna cost you, mister!" the driver said bitterly.

"Don't worry about it." Freddy passed a twenty-dollar bill across the back of the seat, and the driver's fingers snatched it. "Just drive north on Dixie until I tell you to stop."

"Okay," the driver said, "but this twenty's for the cleanup, not for the fare on the meter."

When they reached Dania, Freddy told the driver to stop at a closed Union service station on the highway. Freddy doubled the tab on the meter, but he got no thanks from the grim-faced driver. The cabbie made a U-turn and started back toward Miami without a word.

Freddy's house was twelve blocks from the gas station, a long walk in the rain, but now that he had a Murder One rap hanging over him he sure as hell didn't want the driver to know his address. Jesus, it had all happened so fast. He had gone by the place three or four times when he had cased out the coin dealer, but the man had always been alone in his shop. Who would have suspected that Wulgemuth had a dumb sonofabitch in the storeroom with a shotgun? Well, that was tough shit for Pedro, and tough shit for Wulgemuth—and tough shit for his fingers, too. Susan would be home now, unless she had misunderstood everything he had told her and had driven over to Watson Island and parked in the Japanese Garden parking lot. But she wasn't that dimwitted. Some traffic cop or meter maid had made her move, and she had either circled the block while he was still in the coin shop, or made a second tour of the block and perhaps a third. She might still be downtown, circling the block again and again, but she would give up eventually and drive home to Dania.

Wet all the way through his jacket and shirt, Freddy slogged through the rain with soggy trousers and wet feet. When he got home he would take a Darvon and drink some chocolate milk to settle his stomach. It might be a good idea to get Edna Damrosch to take a look at his injured hand. No, that would mean explanations, and this time she would call a doctor. He would just take some Darvon, some penicillin tablets, and wait till they got to Okeechobee. The pain wasn't all that bad. He could stand a little pain, but those missing fingers would certainly make him a marked man—and for life, too.

The TransAm wasn't parked in the driveway. The stupid little bitch. She was still downtown, circling the block and looking for him. He should have given her a time limit. He needed her right now, and she wasn't home.

He let himself into the house, surprised to see that the lights were still on in the kitchen. He thought he had turned them off when they left. He went into the bathroom, swallowed two Darvons, and sipped some water from the cup on the sink. The door to the closet was standing open. Susan's two suitcases were missing. Her black dress wasn't on the hanger in the closet. He ran into the kitchen, took down the Ritz Cracker box from the back shelf where the provisions were kept, and ripped open the top.

The money was gone. All of it, including the 10,000 Mexican pesos they hadn't been able to exchange. Freddy laughed. So Susan had skipped out on him, taken some of her clothes, the money, and gone home. He had known she was nervous—she told him so—but he hadn't taken into account how truly scared she must have been. Maybe she

193

thought he was going to shoot the coin dealer. Well, as it turned out, she was right.

She must have bolted as soon as he had rounded the corner to Flagler. It was understandable, but unexpected. Now he would have to find his own way up to Okeechobee, track her down, get his money back, and find a way to dispose of her body. He couldn't let her live, not now, not after finding out what he had already known from the beginning—that he couldn't trust Susan; that, in the final analysis, a man couldn't trust anyone. But especially not a whore.

Freddy took Wulgemuth's wallet and the wad of bills from the till out of his jacket pocket. With his good hand, he counted out five twenties and eight tens on the kitchen table. He had another six or seven hundred in his own wallet. Even though he had left the coin case in the shop, he was still ahead in the operation. He wasn't broke, and he still had a shitload of credit cards—

Hoke Moseley stepped through the door to the kitchen from the screened back porch. He pointed his .38 at Freddy.

Freddy turned and stared at Moseley for a long moment, taking in the gray haggard face, the steady pistol, the wet, ill-fitting leisure jacket.

"Raise your hands," Hoke said, "level with your shoulders."

"What'll you do if I don't, old man, shoot me? And what are you doing in my house? Where's your warrant?"

"I said to raise your hands."

Freddy grinned and raised his hands slowly.

"Where's Susan?" Hoke said.

"You tell me, man." Freddy lifted his chin. "I had all my money in that Ritz Cracker box, and she cleaned me out and took off."

"Why'd she take off that way, after she dropped you off downtown on Miami Avenue?"

"Look, my hand hurts, and I've got to get to a doctor. Can I drop my left hand? It hurts like a sonofabitch. You got

194

some crazy people in this town, d'you know that? I go into Wulgemuth's to sell some coins, and the crazy bastard and his bodyguard try to kill me with a damned sugarcane knife. Is that why you're here? I was coming down to tell you about it as soon as I saw a doctor."

Hoke was genuinely puzzled. "What happened in Wulgemuth's?"

"I just told you." Freddy rested his bandaged hand on his chest. "I took some silver dollars down to Wulgemuth's Coin Exchange to get them appraised. If the price was right, I was going to sell 'em. Then him and his bodyguard, a crazy Cuban with a shotgun, tried to rob me. Old man Wulgemuth tried to hack off my hand with a damned machete, and he got most of it, too. I'm hurting, man, and you've got to get me to a doctor!"

"Then what happened?"

"When?"

"After this respectable businessman's unprovoked attack."

"I took a cab home, because Susie wasn't waiting for me any longer, that's all."

"Before that, before you left the store?"

"I got lucky. Before these two crazy people could kill me, I was able to get the gun out of Wulgemuth's drawer and defend myself with it."

"And you shot them?"

"I have no idea. I just started shooting, and when they ducked for cover I ran out. I don't think I hit either one of them. I was just concerned with getting out and finding a doctor, that's all." Freddy moved his feet, inching toward Moseley. Hoke stepped back and extended his arm.

"Back up! Turn around slowly, lean against the wall, and spread your legs."

Freddy shook his head. "I can't do it. I'd pass out. Most of my fingers are gone, and I'm liable to go into shock any minute . . ." Freddy's voice dropped to a theatrical whisper. "Things are going black, all purple and black . . ."

His knees buckled, and as he dropped to the floor, he managed to break his fall with his right hand. He fell over on his left side, groaned piteously, and fished in his jacket pocket for his pistol. As the .38 cleared the pocket, Hoke shot him in the stomach. Freddy screamed and rolled over, trying to get to his feet and get the pistol out of his pocket at the same time. Hoke shot him in the spine, and Freddy stopped moving. Hoke bent down and fired another round into the back of Freddy's head.

Hoke slumped into a kitchen chair and put his pistol on the table. When Bill Henderson, Ellita Sanchez, and Sanchez's uniformed cop cousin from Hollywood came through the unlocked front door, Hoke was still sitting in the kitchen chair, smoking his third cigarette.

23

"YOU OKAY, HOKE?" Henderson asked.

"I'm not hurt, if that's what you mean." Hoke dropped the cigarette on the floor and stepped on it as he got to his feet.

"Stay there," Henderson said. "Sit down." Henderson told the uniformed officer to go out to the front porch, and to prevent anyone else from coming into the house. "You don't have to stay out in the rain, Mendez. Just turn on the porch light, and stand inside the front door."

"Mendez?" Hoke said, starting to get up again.

The officer left the kitchen. "Yeah," Henderson said, "Mendez is Sanchez's cousin, a traffic officer from Hollywood. Why in the hell didn't you wait for us, for Christ's sake?"

Sanchez was on her knees beside Freddy's body. She took a Swiss army knife out of her handbag, opened the small scissors, and started to cut away the bandage on Freddy's left hand. Hoke watched her with keen interest.

"I was afraid he'd get away, Bill. It looked as if he was preparing to leave, and I didn't think I'd have any trouble. I didn't intend to shoot him, but when he went for his gun . . . well . . ."

197

"Did you know he killed Wulgemuth and his bodyguard at the coin exchange store?"

"He said he shot his pistol, but denied hitting anyone. According to him, he was attacked by the two men and he shot back in order to get away."

"Bullshit. It was on the radio. Didn't you have the radio on when you drove after him to Dania?"

"I haven't got a radio. Remember? Somebody stole it when I was in the hospital."

"But you did see him coming out of Wulgemuth's Coin Exchange, right?"

"With a gun in his hand," Sanchez said, looking up with a smile. She raised Freddy's unbandaged left hand. "See? Three fingers missing. When the ME matches them up, Sergeant Moseley'll be credited with a quick solution to a double murder."

Hoke shook his head. "I didn't see him come out of any coin exchange. I was tailing him, hoping to get some probable cause to shake him down. As an ex-felon, if he had a pistol on him, I was going to pick him up. I lost him, and then picked him up again on the corner of Flagler and Miami Avenue."

"Listen carefully, Hoke." Bill took a chair from the table and sat in front of Hoke, looking directly into his eyes. "You're in some jurisdictional trouble if you don't get your story straight. And here's the way you tell it, and this is the way we'll write it up. You were tailing him, yes, and you lost him for a while, right? Then you saw him coming out of Wulgemuth's store and putting a gun into his pocket as he came out. Suspecting him of a robbery, you called Sanchez for backup from Broward County, and then drove here to his house after losing him downtown when he ran away. Isn't that what happened?"

"Something like that."

"No, exactly like that."

"All right. Exactly like that."

"After you called Sanchez and she got a hold of me, we

found out about the killing of the two men. Sanchez called her cousin, and he came here in his own car. We knew you were in danger, so we didn't have time to contact the Broward County sheriff's office, you see. You knew he had a gun because you saw it when he came out of the store. As an off-duty police officer, you went after him and contacted higher authority, through Sanchez."

"I also suspected him of a California assault, and I had reasonable cause to pick him up on that."

"Okay. That's your story. Don't change it. I'll call Captain Brownley and Doc Evans. Brownley'll call the Broward sheriff, and I imagine Doc Evans will contact the Broward County ME. The report's going to be a jurisdictional mess."

"What about the girl?" Sanchez said, joining them at the table. "What's her name?"

"Susan Waggoner," Henderson said. "We'll put out an APB on her. In this rain, she can't get too far away. I'll get out the all-points as soon as I call Brownley."

"D'you want me to call?" Sanchez said.

"No, I'll call. Why don't you make some coffee? This is going to be a helluva long evening."

"I'll make the coffee," Hoke said, getting up.

Sanchez went to the sink, and turned on the tap. "Find the pot," she said. "We'll make it together."

CAPTAIN BROWNLEY AND the Broward County sheriff both made some compromises, and so did the Broward County medical examiner. It was more important to clear up the murders of the coin exchange proprietor and his bodyguard than it was to hold hearings in Broward County. A young lieutenant from the Dania Police Department, who was temporarily in charge while the Dania chief of police was hunting wolves in Canada, was awed by all of the brass from Dade and Broward counties and was willing to do almost anything to get Freddy's body out of town as quickly as possible. In a small town like Dania, shootings of any kind were bad for business.

Susan Waggoner was picked up by a Florida state trooper in Belle Glade. Her TransAm was impounded there, and she was brought to the Miami police station by the trooper. The trooper who picked her up also gave her a ticket for having tinted windows in the TransAm that were twice as dark as the law allowed.

Hoke, Henderson, and Sanchez were still working on their joint report when Susan was brought in. They took her down to an interrogation room, and Henderson read her her rights.

"D'you understand," Hoke said, "that you can have a lawyer present? You don't have to tell us anything if you don't want to, but we need to clear up a few things."

"I don't know what this is all about," Susan said. "When we had the windows tinted on the car, the man said it was legal. You see a lot of people driving around Miami with tinted windows, and a lot of them are darker than mine."

"Never mind the tinted windows," Hoke said. "I followed you in my car from Dania to downtown Miami, and I was across the street when you parked in the yellow loading zone on Miami Avenue. I saw your boyfriend get out of the car—"

"Junior?"

"Junior. And then you took off almost immediately. Did you know he was going to rob the coin store?"

"No. Why would he rob the store? He had some silver dollars to sell. That's what he told me, and he wanted me to go with him. I didn't want to go because of the rain, and when I said I'd stay in the car and wait for him he got mad at me. That's when he told me that he was the one who broke my brother's finger out at the airport. Remember that?"

"He told you that?"

"That's right. And I'll sign a statement to that, too. We'd had some arguments before, and he even hit me once, but I stayed with him because of his other good qualities. But

200

when I found out that he was the one responsible for Martin's death, I got scared. I realized that I was in danger from him, and I got scared. Once he told me that, you see, he'd always know that I had something on him, and he could kill me, too. So I just took off, came home to Dania, got my money, and left. I was on my way back to Okeechobee when the state trooper pulled me over in Belle Glade."

"What were Junior's good qualities?" Sanchez asked.

Susan frowned. She poked out her lips. "Well, he was a good provider, and he liked everything I cooked for him. There were lots of good things about Junior I liked. But I'm not going to live with him anymore."

"Junior's dead, Susan," Henderson said. "Didn't you know he had a gun?"

"Yes, but I didn't know he was going to rob anybody. He carried a gun for protection. He almost got killed a few weeks ago by a gunman in a Seven-Eleven store. So he needed the gun for protection, he told me. Junior's dead?"

"That's right," Henderson said. "He was killed."

"I guess his gun didn't do him much good, then, did it? I'm sorry to hear that. I never wished him any harm. I wasn't going to tell on him, either, about Martin, I mean, but I don't want to get in no trouble on account of Junior. I didn't do anything. I just want to go back to Okeechobee. All I've had is trouble of some kind or other ever since I came down here for my abortion. What I'd say, if you asked me about Miami, I'd say it's not a good place for a single girl to be."

"Jesus Christ," Hoke said, "let's get out of here a minute, Bill."

Hoke and Henderson went out into the hallway.

"I'm afraid, Bill," Hoke said, "that I'd have to confirm her story. She did drop him off, and then leave immediately, and I followed her until she got on the ramp to I-Ninety-five. You can't charge her for dropping her common-law husband off downtown. If she claims she didn't know he was going to rob the store, we can't hold her as an accessory."

"Is she really that dumb, or is it an act of some kind?"

"It's consistent, whatever it is. Why don't we just take her statement and put her on a bus for Belle Glade so she can get her damned car."

"You mean just let her go?"

"I don't see what else we can do. Her statement will clear up the death of Martin Waggoner, and we can always find her if we need her later. Okeechobee's a small town. We'll tell her not to leave Okeechobee or come back to Miami again, and that's it."

"That's just hearsay. We still can't prove that Junior killed Martin, or broke his finger."

"We'll send his picture up to those two Georgia boys. Maybe they can identify him from the picture. At any rate, I'll call the assistant state attorney, and tell her about Susan's statement. She can decide whether to close the case or not. It's not up to us, anyway."

Henderson and Sanchez stayed in the interrogation room to obtain a statement from Susan Waggoner, and Hoke went back to his office. He found Violet Mygren's phone number, and called the office.

"Thank you," a female voice answered, and then, for five minutes, Hoke listened to Muzak as he held the phone to his ear.

"Thank you for waiting," a man's voice said. "How may I help you?"

"Is this the state attorney's office?"

"Yes, it is. How may I help you?"

"This is Sergeant Moseley, Homicide. I want to talk to Miss Violet Nygren, one of your assistant state attorneys. This is the number she gave me."

"I don't think we've got anybody here by that name."

"Yes, you have. She was assigned to that case at the airport. A guy got his finger broke and died from shock. Martin Waggoner."

"I don't know her. What's her name again?"

"Nygren. N-Y-G-R-E-N. She was young and had just joined the office. A UM Law School graduate."

"Okay. Let me take a look at the roster. Can you hold the line a minute?"

"Yeah."

"I'm sorry," the man said, when he came back on the line, "but we don't have any Nygrens on the roster. If you want me to, I'll check with a few people here and then call you back. I don't know half the people here myself. We've got one hundred and seventy-one assistant state attorneys, you know."

"That many? I thought you only had about a hundred."

"We got some more money last year. But they come and go, you know. Want me to check and call you back?"

"No. I'll hold the line while you check. I like listening to the Muzak."

"That's on the other line. I can't get you any Muzak on this phone."

"Never mind. Just find out what happened to Violet Nygren."

Hoke lit a cigarette. He raised his shoulder to hold the phone against his head and examined his hands. They were shaking slightly, as the reaction finally settled in, but as long as he kept busy he wouldn't have to think about it. As he butted the cigarette in the desk ashtray, a woman's voice came on the line.

"Hello? Are you there?"

"I'm here," Hoke said. "Who are you?"

"Tim asked me to tell you about Violet. You are Sergeant Moseley, aren't you?"

"Yes."

"Well, Violet Nygren resigned a few weeks back. She got married, but I don't know her married name. But I know she married a chiropractor out in Kendall, and I can get her married name for you tomorrow, if you like. I didn't know Violet very well, but I know she wasn't happy here as a state

203

attorney. I don't think she'd've been with us much longer even if she hadn't got married and quit—if you know what I mean."

"I think I do. But it's not important. Somebody must've taken over her caseload, so I'll just send a memo over to your office, and you people can take it from there."

"I'm sorry I couldn't be more helpful."

"You've helped a lot. Thanks."

WHEN HENDERSON AND Sanchez went into Captain Brownley's office to go over the written report, Hoke was excluded from the meeting and told that his turn would be next.

Hoke could see the three of them through the smudged glass walls of Brownley's office, and he felt a little apprehensive at being left out. Brownley was a good reader, and if he spotted any discrepancies, Hoke knew that he could be in some deep trouble. Hoke went into the men's room to take a leak and two younger Homicide detectives congratulated him warmly, so warmly that he decided not to go down to the cafeteria for coffee and a sweet roll. As far as his fellow police officers were concerned, the department had won one for a change. The robbery-murder on Flagler and the killing of the suspect would only rate a three- or four-inch story in the local sections of the Miami newspapers, but it was big news within the department.

Hoke returned to his little office and waited, trying to sort out his feelings, and came to the conclusion that Freddy Frenger, Jr., AKA Ramon Mendez, had played out the game to the end and didn't really mind losing his life in a last-ditch attempt to win. Junior would have been good at checkers or chess, thought Hoke, where sometimes a poor player can beat a much better one if he is aggressive and stays boldly on the attack. That was Junior, all right, and if you turned your head away from the board for an instant, to light a cigarette or to take a sip of coffee, he would steal one of your pieces. Junior didn't have to play by the rules, but

204

Hoke did. Nevertheless, Hoke decided to keep this checkers analogy to himself. No matter how he rationalized his actions, Hoke suspected that the real reason he had killed Freddy Frenger was that the man had invaded his room at the Eldorado Hotel and beat the shit out of him. And if he could do it once, he could do it a second time. On the other hand, to think that way was just another oversimplification. After all, Frenger had tried to pull his gun, so Hoke had shot in self-defense: the extra round he had put into the back of the man's head was merely insurance. But any way Hoke looked at it, the quality of life in Miami would be improved immeasurably now that Freddy Frenger was no longer out on the streets . . .

Henderson opened the door. Ellita Sanchez, smiling, was with him.

"Your turn, Hoke," Henderson said.

"We'll wait for you down in the cafeteria," Sanchez said.

Hoke shook his head. "Not in the cafeteria. I don't want a bunch of people coming around." Hoke looked at his wristwatch. "Christ, it's after four A.M. Why don't you guys go home? You don't have to wait for me."

"We'll wait for you in the parking lot," Henderson said. "Then we'll go get a beer."

Henderson and Sanchez left before Hoke could say anything else.

Captain Brownley was on the phone. As Hoke hesitated outside the office, Brownley held up his left hand, signaling Hoke to wait. Hoke lit a cigarette, and tried not to look through the glass door at Brownley. At last, Brownley hung up the phone, stood, and beckoned for Hoke to come in.

"Sit down, Hoke. I see you started smoking again." Brownley sat down, and put his elbows on the desk. Hoke pulled the ashtray toward him as he sat down, and stubbed out his cigarette.

"I never really quit, captain. I just abstained for a while, that's all."

"How d'you feel?"

"Still a little shaky, but I'll be all right."

"I know you will. But for an experienced police officer, that was just about the dumbest trick you ever pulled. Not only should you have waited for backup, but going after a man like Frenger called for a SWAT team."

"I was afraid he was going to get away—"

"That's no excuse. You knew he was armed, even if you didn't know he'd killed Wulgemuth and his bodyguard."

"Maybe I should've waited a little longer, but—"

"Shut up! How in the hell can I chew your ass if you keep interrupting me?" Brownley frowned, took a cigar out of the humidor on his desk, and began to unwrap it.

Brownley's face was creased with thousands of tiny wrinkles. His face reminded Hoke of a piece of black silk that has been wadded into a tiny ball and then smoothed out again. But the captain's cheeks were grayish with fatigue, and there were a few gray hairs in his mustache as well—gray hairs Hoke hadn't noticed before. How old was Brownley, anyway? Forty-five, forty-six? Certainly no more than forty-seven, but he looked much, much older.

Brownley, turning his cigar as he lighted it with a kitchen match, looked at Hoke with unreadable eyes. The whites of his eyes were slightly yellow, and Hoke had never noticed that before either.

"I just got through talking to the chief," Brownley said, "and we made a compromise. I'm going to write you a letter of reprimand, and it'll go into your permanent file."

Hoke cleared his throat. "I deserve it."

"Damned right! The chief, on the other hand, is going to write you a letter of commendation. You might be puzzled by the ambiguity of his letter, but it'll be a commendation. That will also go into your permanent file. So one letter will, in a sense, cancel out the other."

"I don't deserve a letter of commendation."

"I know you don't, but this case'll give the chief something positive to talk about at the University Club next week, and besides, it'll help you out at the hearing. And in a way, maybe you do deserve a commendation from the chief. That was good police work, getting Sanchez to call Ramon Mendez—"

"Who?"

"Ramon Mendez. Sanchez's cop cousin in Hollywood."

"I forgot for a minute. Mendez was one of Frenger's names—"

"I know. But the fact that we had at least one Broward County officer at the scene helped to get us off the hook when we entered Broward's jurisdiction. Because of the seriousness of the crime, we probably would've been okay anyway, but having a Broward officer present helped save a little face. This is politics, Hoke, not police work. I'm sending Officer Mendez a commendation, as well as one for Henderson and Sanchez. And your letter of reprimand will be fairly mild, because the chief just confirmed my majority." Brownley puffed on his cigar. "As of the first of the month, you can call me Major Brownley."

"Congratulations, Willie." Hoke grinned.

"Major Willie." Brownley took a cigar out of the humidor and offered it to Hoke, but Hoke waved it away.

"I'll stick to cigarettes, major. What happens to me now?"

"As you know, there's no standard operating procedure. Usually, when a cop shoots a suspect, we just send him home to wait for the hearing or we give him a desk job while he waits. If the shooting's accidental or if it looks like a grand jury matter, the officer's usually suspended, with or without pay. In your case, as long as you're on sick leave anyway, you just go home and wait for the hearing."

"There's a few things to clear up first. I want to call San Francisco, and—"

"You'll go home and stay there. Don't come into the station until the hearing. You can call Sanchez, and let her clear up any loose ends. Don't talk to the press or to anyone else about the case. You're not going to have any problems at the hearing. Deadly force was justified, and you'll be cleared."

"All right. I'll call Sanchez. She can handle things all right."

"She likes you, too. Of course, when I told you to win her over, I didn't mean for you to prove what a good shot you were, but at least she's not complaining about her supervisor."

"It won't be the same as working with Bill Henderson, but then, Bill can't type eighty-five words a minute, and she can. So I guess it'll even out."

"Get the hell out of here, Hoke. I've still got some calls to make."

Hoke got to his feet. "I'd like to go up to Riviera Beach to spend a few days with my father."

"Okay. Just call in every day. As long's we can reach you by phone."

They shook hands, and Hoke left the office.

WHEN HOKE GOT to the station parking lot, Henderson and Sanchez were waiting for him. The morning air was moist and hot, and Hoke could feel his pores opening. The humid air felt good after the stale air-conditioning of the station, and Hoke didn't really mind the little rivulets of perspiration that rolled down his sides.

Ellita Sanchez had removed her blue faille suit jacket, and her upper lip was beaded lightly with sweat. Henderson's heavy shoulders slumped with fatigue, and his eyes were bloodshot. Hoke knew that neither one of them wanted a beer as much as they wanted a bed, but he also suspected that they were as reluctant as he was to break up a process they had shared, a certain sense of teamwork.

"How'd you make out, Hoke?" Henderson said.

"I'm still on sick leave, but I'm supposed to stay away from the station until the hearing. Brownley said I could go up to Riviera Beach, though, and stay with my father if I wanted to, and I think I will."

"You haven't been up to Riviera for a while, have you?"

"'Bout a year ago, when the old man got married again —remember?"

"Let's go to the Seven-Eleven," Sanchez suggested. "You guys can get a beer, and I'll get a grape Slurpee. My throat's dry, but it doesn't feel like a beer for breakfast."

"Suits me," Henderson said. "We can take my car."

"Let's walk," Hoke said. "It's only a block. We can stretch our legs."

They walked to the 7-Eleven, down the narrow Overtown sidewalk, Hoke beside Sanchez, with Henderson lumbering a few feet ahead of them.

"You ever been to Riviera Beach, Ellita?"

"Never. I've been to Palm Beach, but not to Riviera."

"Palm Beach is right across the inlet from Singer Island, and Singer's a part of the Riviera Beach municipality, with the best beach in Florida. So, if you went as far as the northern end of Palm Beach, you were looking across at Singer. I grew up in Riviera Beach, but I didn't know it was actually called Riviera until I was almost twenty years old. We always called it Rivera. River*a*—that's what everybody called it. Funny, isn't it?"

"I've noticed that a lot of Miamians call Miami Mi-am-ah. I guess it's what you grow up with."

"In Riviera, that's how we can tell the natives from the tourists. Most of us still say Rivera."

When they got to the 7-Eleven, Sanchez asked the manager to fix her a grape Slurpee. Hoke and Henderson went to the freezer. Henderson got a Bud, and Hoke reached deep into the box to get a cold Coors. Each paid for his own drink, and then they went outside to drink them. A few blocks away, in the nascent morning light, they could see the vultures circling above the county courthouse tower, preparing to fly to the city dump for their breakfast feeding.

"That yellow Nova," Sanchez said, pointing to the dusty car parked by the Dempsey Dumpster, "has been there for three days. I remember seeing it."

"Probably the manager's car," Henderson said. "There's no one else around here."

Sanchez walked down to the car. "It's got Michigan plates."

Henderson cracked open the glass door to the store. The manager had *The Star* open on the counter and was reading it. He looked up. "You from Michigan?" Henderson said.

"What?"

"Are you from Michigan?"

"Michigan?" The manager shook his head. "Ponce. In Puerto Rico."

"That your car? The yellow Nova?"

The Puerto Rican shook his head. "My wife's got my car. She drives me to work, and picks me up. That car's been parked there for three days."

"You guys better come down here a minute!" Sanchez raised her voice. She threw her waxed cup, still half full, into the dumpster. Hoke and Henderson joined her at the back of the Nova. "D'you smell anything funny?"

Henderson bent over and sniffed at the trunk. He smiled broadly at Hoke. "Take a sniff, Hoke. Be my guest."

Hoke took a deep sniff at the trunk lid, where it joined the body. The odor was unmistakable; it was the familiar odor of urine, feces, death. Hoke raised his head, returning Henderson's knowing metal-studded smile with a wry grin.

"You two stay here," Hoke said, "I'll walk back to the station and send down a squad car—"

"No you won't," Henderson said. "Go home, Hoke! Just get in your car and go home. We'll take care of the body. You're on sick leave and off duty. Remember?"

"He's right, Hoke," Sanchez said. "It'll be at least another hour before we can run a make and get a warrant to open the trunk. Go on home. Please."

"But I'd like to see—"

"Beat it!" Henderson said, pushing Hoke's shoulder.

"All right. But call me tomorrow, Sanchez. There're a few things—"

"I'll call you," Sanchez said. "But right now you'd better get going."

"You call me, too, Bill."

"I will, I will. Good-*bye*, Hoke."

Hoke returned to the police station parking lot and got into his car. As he drove out of the lot he could see Ellita Sanchez leaning back against the trunk of the yellow Nova. Henderson was probably still in the store, using the manager's phone.

Hoke drove down to Biscayne Boulevard and turned north, hugging the right lane so he could make the cut-off at the MacArthur Causeway for Miami Beach. Feeling slightly guilty about leaving Henderson and Sanchez stuck at the 7-Eleven, he pulled down the visor against the morning sun rising above South Beach and headed for the Eldorado Hotel, where Old Man Zuckerman was waiting for him in the lobby with a fresh, neatly folded paper napkin.

The following news item was published in *The Okeechobee Bi-Weekly News:*

OCALA—Mrs. Frank Mansfield, formerly Ms. Susan Waggoner, of Okeechobee, won the Tri-County Bake-Off in Ocala yesterday with her vinegar pie entry. The recipe for her winning entry is as follows:

Pastry for a nine-inch crust
1 cup seedless raisins, all chopped up
¼ cup soft butter
2 cups sugar (granulated)
½ teaspoon cinnamon
¼ teaspoon cloves
½ teaspoon allspice
4 eggs, large, separated
3 tablespoons 5 percent vinegar
1 pinch of salt

Cream the butter well with sugar. Add spices and blend well. Beat in yolks with a beater till smooth and creamy. Stir in chopped raisins with a wooden spoon. Beat egg whites with a dash of salt until they are soft, then slide onto sugar mixture. Cut and fold lightly but well. Turn into pastry-lined pan. Bake fifteen minutes in pre-heated 425°F. oven. Reduce heat to 300°F. and bake for twenty minutes longer, or until top is beautifully browned and center of filling is jellylike. Cool on a rack for two or three hours before cutting.

When Mrs. Mansfield was handed the prize by the judges (a $50 US Savings Bond), she said, "I never met a man yet that didn't like my pie."

ABOUT THE AUTHOR

Charles Willeford is the author of MIAMI BLUES, SIDE-SWIPE, THE WAY WE DIE NOW, and NEW HOPE FOR THE DEAD, featuring Miami detective Hoke Moseley. He is also the author of SOMETHING ABOUT A SOLDIER and ten other novels.

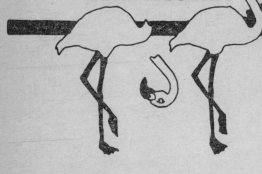